SAVAGE

when cultures collide,

one defines

the civilised

By Courtney J. Scott

Copyright © 2018 by Courtney J. Scott

All rights reserved.

Cover design by Ghanipixels.

Book design by Courtney J. Scott.

No part of this book may be reproduced in any form or by any electronic or mechanical means including information storage and retrieval systems, without permission in writing from the author. The only exception is by a reviewer, who may quote short excerpts in a review.

This book is a work of fiction. Names, characters, places, and incidents either are products of the author's imagination or are used fictitiously. Any resemblance to actual persons, living or dead, events, or locales is entirely coincidental.

Courtney J. Scott

Follow me on Instagram at: allwritescottie

First Printing: November 2018

Independently published

ISBN: 9781729490495

To Jahleel

...still my favourite human

*The Taino names of the Caribbean islands based on Jalil
Sued-Badillo (ed.), 'General History of the Caribbean,
vol. 1: Autochthonous Societies' (Paris: UNESCO
Publishing/London: Macmillan 2003) Plate 8.*

Christopher Columbus' Notes

"They ... brought us parrots and balls of cotton and spears and many other things, which they exchanged for the glass beads and hawks' bells. They willingly traded everything they owned... . They were well-built, with good bodies and handsome features.... They do not bear arms, and do not know them, for I showed them a sword, they took it by the edge and cut themselves out of ignorance. They have no iron. Their spears are made of cane... . They would make fine servants.... With fifty men we could subjugate them all and make them do whatever we want."

- Epistola Christofori Colom, October 12, 1492

Author's Notes

Savage is set on the Caribbean island known by its native Taino people as, Quisqueya; modern day Hispaniola which is shared by the nations of Haiti and The Dominican Republic.

The story spans the period between the arrival of the Spanish in 1492 to just around a decade and a half later when the narrator, Karaya, is seen as a grown woman.

The half Taino, half Castillian narrator weaves together strands of distinct stories that, in fact, define and account for her own existence and life experiences in the new cultural context she finds herself. She occupies a privileged vantage point from which she observes, is told about, or participates in, the events shaping her world.

Karaya's accounts also mirror the narratives that have forged and perpetuated the idea of the discovery, exploration and definition of a whole New World, by enterprising Europeans. This infantilised New World is juxtaposed against the implicitly truth-infused narratives of pre-existence, permanence (and therefore preeminence) within which the notion of the Old World is intentionally situated.

The stories told in *Savage* explore the ironies and subjectiveness of history, notions and assumptions of identity, placement and displacement within imagined class and power structures. These are essentially the themes which have shaped and continue to impact the wider geo-political space where the fictional narratives of *Savage* are located: the Caribbean; the Americas; the entire New World.

Savage is not a history book. The reader is reminded that this is indeed a work of fiction set against a backdrop of echoes and shadows of historical events. History of course holds copious accounts and records about those events as told and remembered by the *conquistador* class.

In the text, the absence of a proper footnoted credit to the "Australian Aboriginal saying" at the beginning of Phase IV, THIS LAND, - "We are all visitors to this time, this place…" – is instructive. All other quotations, at the beginning of each respective

Phase within the narrative, are complete with referencing. Each of the quotes in this respect, is taken from 'recorded historical happenings' where the *conquistador* class identifies the event as historically significant, and therefore records it as such. So-called Australian Aboriginal sayings, and others like those, are perhaps worthy of casual mention, but not deserving of a traceable footnote on the pages of history. It also examines the question of how history is defined: if it's not written, it didn't happen, ergo it's not history.

Perhaps most importantly, the anonymous quote echoes the voice of a resilient people whose words defy accepted norms of history and continue to resound through time.

The Taino people, about whom many accounts and memories have been recorded, had no say in how their stories, or accounts affecting portraits of themselves, have been written or told.

With this in mind, a glossary of Taino words or terms is provided at the end of the text. The glossary is intended to illuminate the narrative but certainly not meant to position the author as an authority on things Taino, or master of the Taino language. After all, a good swoop and trudge through Wikipedia and Google (and other "*serious*" historical texts and records, of course), furnished those definitions and references. If anything, blame them. Or praise them.

It is remarkable that so many words, used in English, Spanish and other modern languages, are borrowed from the Taino lexicon, and largely without credit (or knowledge). Canoe, hurricane, barbeque, papaya, potato, are just a few.

Perhaps the story the reader might be able to tell about her first barbecue, or his first taste of papaya, bears close similarity to Karaya's own reception and retelling of her stories. Accounts based on memories of memories shared with her; stories about stories told to her. Whether the origins of those stories, like that first slice of juicy papaya, are simply accepted and enjoyed or dissected and interrogated with interest, is really a matter of choice.

Enjoy!

SAVAGE

PHASE I

THIS LAND IS OUR LAND

"At night when the streets of your cities and villages are silent and you think them deserted, they will throng with the returning hosts that once filled them and still love this beautiful land." (Chief Seattle, 1854)[1]

---

[1]Excerpt from a speech given by Chief Seattle of the Suquamish and Duwamish peoples, March 11, 1854, at a meeting called by then State Governor Isaac Stevens to discuss the surrender or sale of Native American land to white settlers.

***

My mother's hands never held me. Her arms did. She had no hands. She used to, though. Till the day I was born. The day my father chopped them off. Right, clean at the joints of her wrists; bones, veins and sinews. She used to have beautiful hands; so she told me. Beautifully tattooed and work-scarred. Proud scars. Not the kind of scars that perhaps come immediately to mind; not those kinds that spring a sequence of ugly images and scenes of horror to some minds.

The limits of this, the only language I know, might not allow me to adequately spell it out. But I shall try anyway.

I mean those scars and calluses that come from planting maize and yuca that fed scores of villages and an entire people. Calluses formed from weaving straw baskets that delivered fruit and cradled new-borns. Marks that held the secrets of a proud existence. Scars that told the story of a whole people.

I remember my mother's stories. In her language. But it's only memories which I cannot repeat with exactitude. Well, I don't know how. Not in the way she would, or even could; but I remember though.

In a way, I lost my mother's language at the very moment I lost the touch of her hands. The moment she lost her hands and had me.

She had beautiful hands. Sometimes she'd ask Issi to hold me, even when I was grown. She said Issi had hands like she used to. Issi had tattoos of ibises on both hands. My mother said the ibis was Issi's birth animal. Spirit animal.

The day Issi was born, two scarlet ibises fluttered outside the bohio and then disappeared into the mangrove. The midwife nodded to Issi's mother, my mother's sister, and that was that, my mother used to say. So, when Issi was old enough, her mother brought her to Ayanti's hut.

Issi told me the story. She said she remembered it like yesterday. But somehow, to her, every time she looked at her two fluttering ibises, it always felt like a today.

Ayanti was a healer, a behique. She was wise. She knew all the medicinal plants and could communicate with the spirits of our ancestors. She could make anyone well. Well, if she wanted to. She could make anyone sick as well, but that was not her way; our way, as she would put it.

Ayanti sometimes chose messengers from among our people, if they were lucky enough to get the privilege of taking our questions and requests to those who had gone on before. She was also responsible for the ceremonial burial of first wives whose husbands had transitioned to the land of our ancestors before the wives themselves were ready to go naturally. Issi said men always seemed to need company, either because they were afraid, or lazy, or both, in both life and death.

When Issi and her mother arrived at Ayanti's bohio, she was sitting inside, toward the back of her hut, "To the left I think. Drying maize and yuca, hanging from the roof. She had a red-clay pot with water, and a wicker basket, with huge brown leaves; tobacco I think. I don't remember exactly. But I remember her eyes."

I never met Ayanti, when I was a child. People believed she had returned to the ancestors, before I came along; before my mother lost her hands. People said she had the sharpest, sternest, warmest gaze ever seen. Her eyes were gold like maize peeping through burnished husks. People said when she looked at you, it felt like the morning sun summoning you to wake up. You didn't avert your eyes; just squint as the warmth gently massaged your face into a smile.

She gave Issi a welcoming nod locking eyes with her the whole time. Issi's mother brought Ayanti a few red beads and some annatto paste. She handed them to her with both hands, a show of respect and gratitude. Ayanti nodded and whispered a "thank you my child" without a single blink, still looking into Issi's ibis soul.

"Such a beauty my child. So you've come. Come."

She took Issi's hands. Held them up appraisingly to her eyes, as if scanning them for imperfections.

Ayanti smiled. "Welcome, welcome." They sat down facing each other. Legs folded to support their bodies.

"I should get this fire started, shouldn't I?" she said, bringing the charcoal to life in the middle of their *circle* of three.

She pulled two scarlet ibis feathers from her waistband which was woven from the bark of mahoe, lined with cotton dipped in purple dye.

She closed her eyes for the first time. Issi said it was as if the sun had blinked and all the lights went out.

When the lights came back on, Ayanti handed one feather to Issi and the other to her mother.

"Surrender this to the fire!" She instructed.

They did.

In unison.

The feathers gave off a stench transforming themselves into streaks of greyish white smoke which fluttered skyward, where the ibis took flight, then slowly disappeared. They left a fading aromatic reminder of their physical existence, only a single breath ago.

"The lights went out again."

Ayanti raised her hands reaching to the back of her neck, loosening her hair. "She always wore it in a tight wound knot, for some reason...quite unlike other women...kind of protruded out, strange. Anyway, when she let it out, I was in awe! Hair fell down her face and neck like rain. Black as crows and just as shiny. I guess the only difference is that crows don't really get wet, quite the same way hair does...," mused Issi, in her usual way of wandering off with words.

Ayanti used her left hand to part a window to her face. Her right hand was holding a long thorn which previously held her hair in place. It was the same thorn, Issi told me, that Ayanti had used to gouge out the eyes of two strange men; then used the very same thorn to remove their testicles.

This time she gazed at the thorn and said, "My child, today we scribe your future, so you never forget. The scarlet ibis delivered you to us and today we carve a reminder on your precious hands. We grow old and forget. Or change our minds. This is your protection against all that business of forgetting or changing of minds."

Ayanti removed the thorn from the hot coals, looked at Issi and said, "This is going to hurt. Ready?"

"Ready!" Issi nodded.

When Issi and her mother, my mother's sister, left Ayanti's hut that day, Issi wore two ibis on her hands and big smile on her face. Ayanti stood at the entrance of her *bohio* to see them off, still wearing that ethereal countenance. There was something new in her expression though. Issi called it shock, and swore she heard Ayanti whisper under her breath, as they fluttered off like ibis in the distance, out of earshot, "Hmmm this one is special. Not even a frown. Not even a wince. No tears. Unbelievable!"

***

"There was blood everywhere," she would say whenever I asked.

"More blood than when you were born. On that full moon, by the river. But blood is life and blood is death," my mother would say.

My mother told me my father chopped off her hands, both of them, the very night I was born. That was the blood of death.

The blood of life oozed me out of her, into the world. In a gush, almost as if life was in a hurry to meet me, she'd tell me. She said I glistened in the blueish brightness of the full moon light. I wasn't blue though. I was pink like a baby *jutia*, a rodent, my mother would tell me with a smile: "Pink and bloody."

She didn't cry when she delivered me, all by herself. All alone. I cried though. That made her heart cry, as she pondered in that very moment of my birth, the best option to help me escape this place where she knew my crying would never end. She wanted to end it, for me, before it begun and continued, forever. Forever is a long time my mother said. Like her life, before it ended.

Before Paco, my brother, slipped her a poisonous potion of bitter yuca, which of course, made her forever end, leaving me no other choice but to kill him.

My mother held me for a moment to comfort me, and comfort herself too, to stop us both from crying. Then in the moments she spent staring at the full moon reflecting on the stillness of the river, rippling like tears on a leaf, her hands wrapped the bloody cord that still connected me to her, around my cuddly soft, turtle-like neck. Her tattooed hands, she told me, started tightening into a grip, as she begun to whisper, "*Taicaraya,* my baby" goodbye, to me, forever. In her language.

My father's dogs found her and me.

He appeared like a shadow on his black stallion. Silhouetted like one of one of the four horsemen of the Apocalypse he had told my mother about when he introduced her to his god and the words of his god. Words which were never spoken, only written in that book that my father told my mother was all truth and not a shred of lie. That was when my mother also learned about lies, from my father and his god of truth.

Las católicas majestades, from a faraway land called Castillia, had sent my father to my mother's land. That was the story my father told my mother. She told me she found it a bit odd, sometime later when she realised that it didn't make much sense to send someone to a land that no one from the other land even knew existed. My mother said it would be as if Cacique Biautex, the supreme leader of my mother's people, before my father's people cut his throat while he slept, were to sail from our beloved Quisqueya to meet another Cacique in Xamayca, but wasn't exactly sure the other Cacique, or Xamayca, for that matter, even existed. It was all a bit odd. Something, she felt, did not add up.

Biautex was the leader of our people before the strange men came. He was great hunter and seaman. He built some of the best canoes and travelled the seas to trade fish, food, gold and ornaments for our people. My mother said he studied and knew weather patterns and could predict the coming of hurricanes. He also knew when to plant or not plant certain crops.

The day the big canoes of the people with pink skin from faraway came, Biautex was out with some other hunters looking for game for the villages. One of the watchmen who looked out for boats from our other peoples, be they friend or foe, ran to fetch Biautex and the hunting men. The watchman knew that the three large canoes that had tall white wings that flapped in the wind, like giant seagulls, were not the canoes of our friendly neighbours from Xamayca, Boriken or Kuba. And they were not the canoes of the savage Kalinago raiders either.

My mother said that Biautex ordered a lavish feast for the strange men. Biautex thought the men looked famished and fatigued and he, like the others, thought their skin needed some nourishment to become normal and brown again.

The feast was like any other *Areito* our people would have had to welcome caciques from other lands or territories. Like the last one before this one, my mother said, when Chief Guaybana came looking for a new wife among our people. He and Biautex believed that a royal marriage between our peoples would help to deepen and preserve our friendship for many moons to come.

Biautex sat on his wood carved ceremonial stool, a duho, and held his tall wooden staff in his right hand. The staff was adorned with pink conch shells, strips of gold and a smooth lightning stone sat on top, glistening like a star. Women performed dances and ballads and filled the courtyard with song, movement and colour. Their feather adorned costumes shimmied like robins in a preening ritual.

Our men could always be counted on never to be outdone. They mainly performed a dance of mock ballgames, *batu*, to the beat of drums and maracas. Each movement, each punch in the air, each swing of the hip, was profoundly exaggerated. Drum. Up. Drum. Down. Drum. Left. Right. Thrust. Drum.

Our people offered the strange men many gifts: gold; pearls; shells; birds; cotton; annatto.

The strange men lived among our people for six full moons, my mother said, before everything changed, forever. She said Biautex even took some of them to show them the sea routes to other lands, like Xamayca and Boriken. They went on hunting expeditions together and they even got plots of land to build their own new huts. In return, the strange men taught our people about swords and horses and god and *las católicas majestades*.

On the sixth full moon, my mother said, the strange men said Quisqueya now belonged to: *las católicas majestades*. "This land is our land!" they declared.

Like the breaking of one of Ayanti's trances, my father's shouts, amidst the cacophony of barking dogs, "*Qué has hecho, salvaje loca?!*" brought my mother back to her forever.

"What have you done, crazy savage!"

She told me it was like being held hostage, wide awake, in a nightmare. The tail of my father's whip landed across her face and for the first time after giving birth to me, she bellowed like a wounded animal. The lilies tattooed on her hands wilted as she lost grip of my lifeline, and I fell back, into life, making a narrow escape from the gateway of death. My father's whip saved my life.

Someone had to nurse me, my mother said, so my father allowed her to live. To teach the others a lesson and for my mother to see the evil savagery of her ways and for her to become a civilised person, according to my father, he chopped off both of her hands.

"There was blood everywhere…"

***

On the morning we became the property of the faraway *majestades católicas*, some men ran to Biautex's hut to share the strange news with him. He was still in his hammock.

Still. Cold. Dead.

Blood thick as annatto paste wrapped around his neck, like the wrinkled cloth the strange men wore around theirs.

My father and his men rounded up all the men of our villages and put them to work searching for gold. Some were worked to death. Some were killed for sport. Or just killed for the simple fact of being.

The strange men took our women. If anyone tried to resist they had to deal with the sharpness of swords splitting them in areas where nature had already started the job. That was the fate that befell Issi's mother. In her protest to protect her dignity, she was prodded and pierced by six penises and climactically penetrated by a cold, compact sword of steel.

My mother said they might have lost their defences, but they were never defenceless. She told me how one night, two strange men raided a hut where Ayanti and the grieving wife of a chief were staying, preparing maize gruel and cakes over an open flame. The chief's wife had lost her two sons and the chief himself. The chief, incidentally, happened to be her second husband. She had dismissed the first man after a spell of what she had described as boredom. It was normal for our women to do that, my mother said.

That evening both women were in the hut reminiscing about the days of not so long ago and plotting ways in which they might regain control of their livelihood and basic survival. Two strange men, rubicund from sunburn, barged into the hut to demand and exact what they seemed to have developed an insatiable appetite for. A thirst, some might say.

"Get on the floor, bitches!" said the taller stranger.

His words filtered out from his lips in a hiss; his upper jaw was missing a pair of front teeth. He was sweating profusely and Ayanti told someone who told my mother later, that he shared the odour of rotting crabs, just like those graceless pink-hoofed gifts the strange men had brought our people when they first arrived. Pigs.

The two strange men had swords which they brandished like near starved hunters who had grown weak, impatient, but most of all, rabid, after the fruitless pursuit of some stubborn prey. They threatened to wedge their swords in crevices where they would have ideally preferred to stick their anguine masculine appendages which had already started to slither and protrude through their skin tight, worn-out, mud clad trousers.

Ayanti, my mother said, was schooled in the art of snake charming. She could charm anything with those eyes. This time though, her charms got the strange men's serpents more than a little rattled and throbbing for prey.

"On the floor bitches!"

Ayanti eyed her grieving widow companion and she followed Ayanti's eyes to the floor. They both coiled onto the floor.

Ayanti looked at her companion again and started to make gyrating motions summoning the widow to follow suit. Her enchanting eyes invited the taller of the two strange men to join in their festive display of sensuality.

"Told you these whores only good for one thing!" said the shorter, stockier man.

He had a limp and a slightly crooked nose which slanted to the left. Ayanti thought he looked as though he had fallen on his face at birth, when the midwife perhaps failed to catch him. Or, perhaps his mother had dropped him when she caught glimpse of the uncute wonder she had released into this beautiful world. In any case, Ayanti thought the damage had already been done and perhaps it now fell to her to rid the world of this one scourge, as well as the other.

Ayanti looked across to her companion to her left, held her gaze, and both women laid still. Opened their legs. Arms up. Hands at the sides of their heads, playfully twirling errant strands of hair.

The strange men grinned, masquerading a rictus of stained and toothless smiles. They started to unbuckle their belts and lower their trousers. Ayanti thought this was taking much longer than what she was accustomed to with her men; they were not lumbered with so many layers of garment to undo. The strange men were wild with excitement, toothily grinning like dead fish, the kind our fishermen would bring ashore after a long day at sea. They didn't bother to remove their trousers all the way. The trousers remained draped around their ankles. They fell to their knees, each trying to straddle one gyrating and seemingly willing conquest.

Ayanti struck first. She reached for the massive thorn which she used as a hair pin, from the back of her head. And in a split second, the thorn had taken root in the right eye of the taller strange man who had the stench of swine. She swiftly transplanted the thorn into the left eye of the shorter strange man, slightly missing the cheek of her widowed companion who had her teeth firmly locked onto the crooked nose of the strange man wailing in agony, flapping on top of her.

By the time the widow could have disposed of the mouthful of flesh and blood dripping down her cheeks, Ayanti had already, with great celerity, successfully repeated the skilful flourish of her weapon. Right. Left. The strange men were howling and writhing in pain, flailing on the floor, grabbing the bloodied sockets their eyes once occupied. Sadly, for the shorter of the two strange men, he only had two hands. He had nothing left to grab his remaining half of a nose, which was streaming a crimson river of blood.

The women were on their feet looking down at the strange men who laid there painting the brown earthen floor with foamy scarlet lathers of blood.

Ayanti's iguana tattooed hand was still glued to her hairpin. Her eyes fierce and piercing like the midday sun. She and her companion were breathing heavily, deeply, steadily. Her eyes darted towards the private parts of the two strange men. The thorn followed, and that was that.

***

My father raised me. Just as he had raised his pigs and tried to breed the four horses that accompanied him on his ship. He told me he was good with animals. His father and mother and brothers and sister, back in the faraway land, had animals on what my father called a farm. He grew up with animals, he liked to say.

After I was born, my father delivered me in his arms to the hut behind his house and thrust me into Issi's arms.

"I trust she will be in safe hands, away from that savage!"

She took me from him without a word.

She just planted herself, feet apart, staring coldly into the grey eyes of Don Joaquin de los Lobos. She rooted herself in defiance against the looming stature of a man who stood in front of her, sword in hand, priding himself a conqueror.

"Stop staring at me, you blinking whore!" Issi laughed as she recounted the episode, mimicking the thundering voice of Don Joaquin.

She had a howl for a laugh. Her whole body would shake like leaves on a windy day. Her eyes would squeeze into a squint and her lips would stretch to form the thinnest of frames, housing and exposing a perfectly formed string of pearly white teeth. Sometimes I thought she had too many teeth.

"It would be funny if I were blinking at all. Blinking! What does that even mean?" she'd cackle off into a frenzy.

From the night I was delivered to Issi's hut, which was also my mother's hut, she protected me like her own child. She had been living together with my mother since the day they were both taken captive by my father. Their duties were to do what captives did; service for, and at, the pleasure of the captor. Issi looked after me and my mother. She held me to my mother's breasts when I was hungry. She cleaned and dressed my mother's wounds with digo until they completely healed, forming pointy stubs that marked the spots where her hands used to be.

Issi told me that nothing was the same after most of our men were killed or forced to work like drones, only not as happy as drones, whose singular gratification came from working themselves to death for the pleasure of their queen.

Lobos took over the best lands and shared them between himself and *las católicas majestades.* Land that produced maize and yuca.

Our people used to share the crops and food our women grew near to the village huts. Under Lobos, they were not allowed to even eat until told to do so – as and when decided by the new landlords. As a result, many of our women and their children died of starvation. Some, Issi told me, poisoned themselves just to escape the new order of things.

Escape was what most of our people lived for, then. Only not everyone was as lucky as Ayanti and the widow. In the dead of night, after the death by thorn of the two strange men who tried to invade their feminine enclaves, both women never stopped running until they reached the roaring, foaming waterfalls, high up in the mountains where the ancestors watched over our land. Issi said Ayanti and the widow lived up there among some others of our people, ones who did not make offerings to the supreme creator Yúcahu Maórocoti, but they were still our people.

After the strange men killed Biautex and buried my mother's father and brother alive, and after Issi's father was sent to sea, she and my mother tried to run away into the hills. They picked a day that, to them, was reminiscent of a time when life was normal. A time of day when everything was still still; when huts would be crowded with sun drunk mothers and children, and hammocks would sway in the stillness, under the weight of snoring men.

That day like in normal times, the sun was high in the sky; hot as yuca baked on red hot coals. That day, while the strange men, exhausted from the unrelenting heat, took refuge slumbering under the shade of trees and in the caverns of huts, Issi and my mother, hand in hand, casually walked out of the village. Then they ran. But as

Issi put it, tired feet were no match for the beastly pursuit of dogs and horses ridden by the strange men.

The strange men caught up with Issi and my mother, and they were re-captured.

"When the rope lassoed and coiled around my body, I was tugged back to reality. From the futile fantasy of freedom," said the saddest words, I had ever heard from Issi's lips, up to that point at least.

The rope gripped their naked torsos, grating off curled up layers of brown skin dabbed with red traces of freshly clotted blood. The rope tightened around them, quite like the grip of foolhardy men catching coconuts hurled from the tallest palms, just for sport.

"We flew backwards through the air. Bruised and bloodied… right in front of stomping hooves!"

***

Don Joaquin de los Lobos told me to call him Don Jota. His other child, his son, who came with him on his ship from the faraway land, called him Papa. Everyone called the son, Paco. Paco called me Lilia, the name my father gave me. He named me after the tattoos my mother once had; lilies. My mother never called me by that name. For her, the name my father gave me represented a sinister form of torture from which Don Jota derived immense pleasure. My mother called me Karaya, which meant moon, in her language.

The number of moons that my mother had been held captive by Don Jota, by the time I was born, was nearly four times the number of all my fingers on my two hands. I had ten. Some of our people had twelve.

Don Jota made concubines of my mother and Issi and others as he pleased. My mother said that meant they were his servants and play things. She said he had a special liking for her, because, according to Don Jota, she presented quite regally, and he wanted a queen. He told her stories about his beautiful queen Isabela and her equally beautiful courtesans. He used to lick his pink lips as he described their skin.

He said their skin was white like ibis and smooth as the inside of conch shells. He said they had golden locks, gold as the sun. And he said they had full, rounded foreheads, not flat like my mother's people's. He would spend days dreaming of the day he would return to his wonderful Castillia, wealthy, propertied and titled. He lamented the path he said had to take to achieve the greatness he said he knew he was destined for, back in his faraway land. He would curse this primitive place, as he called our land, where he had to dwell among the wretched, as he called our people. But he would always sport a self-satisfied smile at the end of each rant, reciting, "Indeed, this is a means to an end...a very necessary evil."

My mother said that sometimes when she spent the night in his hut, he would ask her to hold him while he sobbed and cried himself to sleep.

Usually he would shiver and whimper, "I am a good man! I am! I am not a bad person...I really don't mean to hurt anyone."

That was when he would gasp as if taking his last breath, before he fell deeply asleep. My mother would watch him sleep, sigh and snore. She would recount the stories to Issi who advised her to brew some special cohoba tea, from the seeds of the cojobana tree.

"That will make him sleep better...sound. Don't make it too strong though, or else he might never wake up...," giggled Issi.

"I'm not trying to kill him, you know."

"Like that would be such a terrible thing!"

Cohoba was the same brew the fishermen used to use to trap fish in ponds and rivers. The fishermen would put a bit of the hallucinogen in the water to stunt the fish, so they would sleep or float around in a trance. Then after a moment, the fish would be ready for dinner.

One evening after Don Jota was served his dinner with maize wine, he summoned my mother to his room to help him get ready for bed. My mother said this was usually a euphemism for other servile duties required. She used her stubs of hands to wipe him down with wet, clean cotton rags and did the same to herself. My mother had been forbidden by my father to take baths in the nearby river the way she and my people were accustomed to, every sunrise and sunset. He said the practice was primitive, his favourite word. He said that no queen of his would continue in animalistic traditions after he had been so kind as to teach her the ways of the civilised.

He insisted, as a matter of fact, that no one was ever allowed to bathe in public, in river, pond or sea, again and that all women should cover their whole bodies in cotton dresses, as civilised people back in Castillia did.

That night, after washing and ablution, my mother offered Don Jota some of the special cohoba brew that Issi had advised her to prepare for him. He was in high spirits after his dry clean and gentle shoulder massage, so he was more than delighted to accept any offering presented nicely to him. After all, he was being waited on and treated like the king he knew he had surely become.

That night he started falling asleep before a single thought of any extra bedtime activity had a chance to bud, let alone take root, in his mind. He fell into a semi-stupor making him keen to have any conversation or field any question thrown in his direction. My mother gently massaged his balding head. His head was matted with thin strands of greyish black hair, interspersed with scaly pinkish patches of sunburnt scalp. It resembled some sort of ailment that my mother never really had the words to define.

As Don Jota sunk deeper and deeper into his slumber, a smile curled at the corners of his mouth, ruffling the bristly greyness of his bearded face. It was at that instance, with a tenderness that my mother said she sometimes felt for the strange man, my father, she smiled back and whispered, "Why do you think you are bad, *querido?*"

***

Paco was twelve years old when he set sail along with Don Jota and the other sixty-six strange men who left Castillia in search of new lands, in three ships, to claim them for *las católicas majestades.*

He spoke in sighs, usually with a distant gaze, looking up and out, at nothing and no one in particular.

Sometimes when Paco told me stories, I got the feeling that he was not exactly speaking to me, but in a way, he was speaking to himself. A self which was not exactly present with the self that sat in front of me, or the self that laid in the hammock with arms spilling over, hands playing in my hair sometimes, as I sat sprawled on the floor playing with a grasshopper or something else.

I didn't sense that Paco was sad about his stories, but he wasn't happy either.

"We left Castillia under a cloud of humiliation…but I guess I never felt as disgraced as I initially did, after meeting the others who sailed with Papa and me. They weren't exactly good company, but Papa told me it was better that, than rotting in prison waiting to be hanged."

It was thanks to the mercenary kindness of the wealthy merchant and servant to *las católicas majestades*, Don Ruben, that Paco and Don Jota managed to escape execution and got the chance at a new life in this new land. Plus promised social elevation when they would both eventually return to Castillia.

He didn't really miss Castillia that much, he told me. At least here in Quisqueya he could eat whatever and whenever he liked. He also proudly declared that it was less trouble dealing with women here as he could have any one he wanted without the bother of having to marry any of them, even though he was a man of twenty-two.

In Castillia, because of his god and his faith, he would have likely been married already, to only one wife, he said, and he imagined that must be quite boring for any man, let alone a man of twenty-two! I said perhaps it might also be boring for any woman as well, and I told him the story that Issi told me about the widow who had asked her first husband to leave, because he bored her, or she was bored of him. One or the other.

Paco always seemed very fascinated by the customs of my people, before Don Jota and his people changed them. He was especially thrilled about the practice where a man could have as many wives as the number of fingers and toes he possessed. I would always hasten to remind him of the caveat, that that did not apply to those with two extra fingers or toes, though. We would both laugh, and he would give me a gentle push on the shoulder, muttering "loca". I would push back with "ciguato," which meant the same thing, in my mother's language. "Careful Papa doesn't hear you!" he would say, then we'd laugh some more.

You see, Don Jota did not want me to speak my mother's language. "No language of savages for my little lily!" In fact, I was not allowed to get any tattoos and the thing that broke my mother's heart the most, even more than the fact of our being alive and living under Don Jota's roof, was my punishment of, and life sentence to, ugliness.

My mother's people were beautiful in every way. But one thing that really accentuated their physical beauty was their flattened foreheads. As soon as a newborn's neck was strong enough to bear the weight of its own head, my mother's people would tie a flat piece of wood on its forehead, so it gradually forms the skull at a beautifully sloping angle from brow to the top of the forehead. My forehead was rounded and ugly. Just like Don Jota's. But my mother and Issi still told me I was beautiful, if just a little ugly, they would sometimes tease.

Courtney J. Scott

"So, Paquito, tell me, why do you men want women so badly? I will never understand these things."

"One day you'll be old enough to understand, loca Lilia," he replied, ruffling my curls.

At that he hopped out of the hammock and broke into a sprint, "Catch me if you can! I have to go see after those lazy miners, they should be back by now."

When I told my mother about my day spent with Paco, about how he helped me pick the beans and laid them out to dry and how much fun we had telling stories and me trying to sing ballads in her language, she just absently replied that next time I should do my work by myself or ask Issi to help me and I should stop dreaming and let Paco be.

***

I liked my brother though. I loved him and his stories.

44

When Paco was little, he told me, he and his friends stole bread from a man he called the baker, *señor panadero*. He said bread in the faraway country was quite like our maize or yuca bread, except theirs was white and soft and made from something he called wheat.

They went into the bakery under the guise of selling a black tomcat to the baker. Paco said that cats were good at catching mice. He said that they suspected that the mice were the baker's secret assistants, adding their own ingredients to the bread. The baker would knowingly sell the "special" bread to customers who perhaps knew but were usually too hungry to even bother complaining.

"You mean they'd just eat the shit…?"

"Either that or starve…"

"Can't imagine…"

"You think we had loads of options, Loca? Not like we could just go pick a fruit and eat, like you lot!"

Using the cat, they reckoned, would be a sure way to get something in their stomachs that day.

The baker seemed interested in the deal and Paco perfected his pitch describing the skills and exploits of their feline merchandise.

"This cat's got some serious skills, *señor panadero*! Could catch rabbits if you let it."

"Hmmm, not so sure I can afford it then."

"Would be bad luck to let this bargain slip. Wouldn't be doing yourself any favours letting this one go…"

"Hmmm, poor thing will be bored here…at least he'll be well fed…"

"Indeed…."

"How much did you say it was?"

While he was busy enticing the baker to take the cat off their hands, Paco's other two friends snuck behind the baker and swiped a loaf of fresh bread off the shelf. They snapped it in half and each boy tucked a half loaf under his shirt. The bread was still quite warm and so started to tingle their skin.

The boys could no longer remain quiet. Warmth turned to fire against their skin. They scurried like mice, trying to escape clinging to their only hope of a meal before dinner, that day. The baker tried to grab hold of the boys but Paco, swift on his feet, dived between the baker's loaf-like legs, flipping his apron in the air, covering the baker's face, blocking his vision. The boys made a hasty escape. They left the baker shouting and swearing, spinning in circles like a dizzy dancer who had had too much wine to drink at the *Areito*.

***

My mother could sing better than any bird I had ever heard. And I heard many.

Because she was forbidden to speak to me in her language, after she had learned Don Jota's language, like all her people were forced to do, she would sing to me in her language. And whenever Don Jota or anyone challenged her, she would simply ask, "How can my songs make sense in words I don't even own? Would I be singing or just making noise?" They would let her sing.

She and Issi would sing and dance to entertain and educate me in our hut at night, the times when we would finally be alone together and neither of them had to be alone with Don Jota. Their ballads carried tales of our people. They would sway their hips in the smoothest most fluid of motions. Left, right, around.

They taught me the moves of the batu, the ball game our people used to play in the ceremonial courtyards known as the batey. Those days, playing was no longer allowed. Don Jota said our people were too lazy and needed to be kept busy working in the fields and mines. They could do anything on land, but no fishing at sea in canoes or on rafts since that was a risk not worth taking. He feared that our people might flee and never return.

Issi dressed me up in feathers and made me sit with my back against the centre-pole of our hut, where the hammocks were tied and spread out to the corners of the rounded hut, like a spider's web.

Our leaders used to sit on their ceremonial stone or wooden duhos, chairs which had the highest backs. Players would compete in the batu while the leaders and our people watched in celebration of the maize of yuca harvest.

They told me Biautex would oftentimes break with tradition to participate in the ballgames as he wasn't much of a type to just sit and be a spectator. He understood his role, and everyone already knew he was our supreme leader, he would say. So, it was not clear to him why he should sit out all the fun! Besides, he was the best batu player bar none!

The way my mother and Issi would talk about Biautex made me wonder whether there wasn't much more to their stories. They said he was agile, muscular and handsome. His hair was long at the back, down to his shoulders. It was cropped at the front and sides – enough to expose the regal beauty of his strong, perfectly

49

flattened and angled forehead. They said he had the warmest soul and therefore the most wives.

I asked my mother if she had wanted to be one of Biautex's wives, and both women all but collapsed with laughter. My mother stopped laughing for an instant and grew silent. It felt as though that were to have been a moment where she would have likely taken my hands in hers, as our women often did. Instead, she sighed deeply and sat down next to me on her folded legs. She looked up at Issi, and Issi sat down too.

My mother told me about Hayuya. "He was the loveliest man I have ever seen in my life."

Hayuya was a cacique from another territory. Perhaps a couple days journey from our village. My mother said he would have been no match for Biautex in a batu competition, but if there were ever to have been a wife-wooing competition, Hayuya would have been the champion, hands down!

He was a craftsman and an artisan. He was responsible for all the stoneworkers and carvers among his people. He made the best Cemis and other ceremonial and religious ornaments.

One evening after a yuca harvest festival where my mother performed a ballad-dance combination, that she had created herself, Hayuya bowed his head toward her and smiled at her. Performing in front of large crowds did not bother my mother in the least. I would even say she relished it. But one look of approval from Hayuya, one targeted smile, hit her so hard that her feet gave way under the light weight of her heart.

She smiled at me and Issi held my hand. My mother looked down at the earthen floor of our hut and let a tear roll from her eye straight unto the dirt. It formed a round crystal of dancing dust.

She looked up at me again and said, "That was the first time I knew I had love that was not for my own father or brothers. I looked at Hayuya and loved him."

***

Paco never liked to talk about his mother. He said it made him sad. I didn't like to press him or bother him when he was in one of his sad, quiet, reflective moods. On occasion when I misread his mood he would erupt and slap me like thunder on a clear day. He would shout at me "Basta, loca Lilia!" I knew "loca", in those moments didn't have the same meaning as the days when I would tickle him and watch him go red and hysterical with laughter. I preferred the Paco of those times.

This one time though, he was in the mood to talk. It was the middle of the dry season and the days were long and scorching hot. Days like these, my mother said, were days they would spend by the river or the sea, wading and splashing till sunset. But that was then.

Now, Paco was red-faced and sweating more than normal, in my view anyway. He had a gourd in his hand, overhanging the hammock as he liked to do. I was walking by about my chores when he hollered, "Loca Lilia, come sit with me!" Before I could summon an excuse, remembering my mother's counsel, he volleyed back, "I don't wanna hear it, get over here, come talk with your brother!"

I sat down under the shade, beside the hammock, my usual spot. "Good, now that's better. What have you been up to anyway?"

Again, I didn't get a chance to start, let alone finish, my reply before Paco started slurring words, between huge sips and swigs from the gourd he had in his hand. Sitting there on the ground with his hand close to my face, I caught a whiff of the contents of the gourd, and as I had suspected, highly fermented, super-potent, maize wine.

"You know Loca, this wine right here, reminds me so much of the tavern I last saw my mother."

He chuckled, at the same time trying to stifle a hiccup, or the hiccup trying to stifle him, it all seemed funny as I recall. I said nothing. I had learned his ways and moods of communication. This was another Paco conversing with Paco situation, so I knew my place. Just keep quiet and listen.

The men in his village back in Castillia met almost every evening at the local tavern to watch their sorrows slowly drown in bottles of sherry and wine. The men he said, would talk about women, money and god. I didn't exactly understand the entirety of what he meant with those words, but I pretended as if I did and said, OK. I also thought these sorrows must have been either so many or so resilient, so much so that they had to keep trying to drown them, evening after evening. I thought then, of earthworms I used to play with and try to kill. With each cut of worm, the same cut piece took on a life of its own and would never seem to die. It was as if I had created more worms out of one. And that scared me sometimes.

He told me his mother worked as a housekeeper for the owner of the tavern and for a long while Don Jota had suspected that his wife, Paco's mother, Angustia, was doing more than just housekeeping for the tavernkeeper. He suspected her contract included many other reasonable duties, mutually agreed, of course.

Paco said that evening Don Jota made him stand on his shoulders at the back of the tavern. That way he could see through the windows into the upstairs living quarters of the tavern. Paco told me that he saw his mother and the tavernkeeper in the tavernkeeper's bed and it was as though they were trying to create as much work as possible; a perfect reason to make up the bed when they were through. That way, said Paco, his mother could perhaps feel justified as a housekeeper, earning her keep helping her worthless drunk of a husband, put bread on the table.

When he descended from Don Jota's shoulders, Paco said the shock printed on his face told his father much more than any words could have possibly expressed. Don Jota grew scarlet red, pacing and stomping about frantically like a mad bull. "Okay boy, we'll wait here! That bastard is going pay!"

It was a cold long wait.

Paco said it felt like the eternity that their priest spoke about when he spoke about unending torment waiting for those who did not obey his god, when they died – except that day it was cold, not hot like the priest described. That sounded very scary to me. I always imagined what Paco called eternity as the time we get to be with the ancestors and never ever leave again. To me, it was the crossover into a happier place, and only happier because those I loved would be there and not die, again. But I was still not sure if Paco meant what I had understood. I kept listening.

"That long wait, Loca, was the beginning of our journey to this place," he slurred on.

"When the men came to arrest Papa, I was kneeling frozen and freezing, with blood on blood on my hands."

He froze next to the lifeless body of his mother who had suddenly stopped breathing in one hollow gasp.

He said her eyes were wide open as if in shock or surprised at what had happened right before her eyes, just moments before.

Paco said it might also have been a sign of the shock Angustia felt as Don Jota's dagger grinded against her pelvic bone, like teeth on edge, as his dagger opened wide, unnecessary windows to her insides. Her hands clutched her abdomen and she looked up into Don Jota's eyes. She fell to her knees, then flat on her face.

"I must have blacked out in that instant. Because I truly do not remember how I got over to my mother's side, on my knees, even," said Paco, speaking to Paco.

"Before I realised that Mama was dead, I was standing there holding the tavernkeeper from behind…he was dead…too."

The moment he heard the thud of his mother's body hitting the rough cobbled stones, he turned around and quickly let go of the death heavy corpse of the tavernkeeper.

"I pounced on him like a fox on a hen! He didn't see me coming and neither of them expected it."

The tavernkeeper was stunted by surprise, so although he was much taller than Paco at the time, Paco had gained the upper hand in making the crucial first strike. He grabbed the tall wiry tavernkeeper from behind as he and Angustia walked out discreetly from the tavern, fulfilling their pleasantries of thank yous and good-byes.

With the lover firmly locked in Paco's embrace, Don Jota swiftly fed him a volley of blows to the face, abdomen and groin. Don Jota got more and more enraged as he punched his helpless rival, and with each plea for mercy from the lover, Don Jota got more and more infuriated. He was overcome by his lust for blood, said Paco, when he suddenly, in blind rage, pulled his dagger from his side and planted it firmly in the tavernkeeper's jugular. He made gargling sounds like water being sucked through a blow hole. Then he went limp like a fish that had given up on the idea life out of water.

"So, Lilia, you see, that was the last time I saw my mother. And I can't even remember if I'm remembering it well."

***

The time had come for Don Jota to make his voyage back to his faraway home. This was his first trip back since he had successfully discovered our lands and our people who had been living there for thousands of years before the fate of Don Jota's discovery. It was his first return but not the first for the three ships that he first arrived with. Those had long returned and now returned with company; more ships, more men, more pigs, more weapons.

Don Jota told Paco that now that he had completed ten years in service to his king and queen and to Don Ruben, he had to go back to secure his freedom from his own, or rather, their own bondage.

After Don Jota murdered his wife and the tavernkeeper, both he and Paco were arrested and charged, one as murderer and the other as co-conspirator. They were both sentenced to prison to await execution.

In his benevolence, Don Ruben Spinoza del Soto, struck a deal with the de los Lobos and the magistrates who had sentenced the pair to death: in exchange for their freedom they were to sail in Don Ruben's ships, in the name of *las católicas majestades*, to find new lands, gold, riches and treasures. They were to serve a bond of ten years, during which time they could live in peace and freedom, but all new-found wealth would belong to the monarchs and Don Ruben, only. After their bond was spent, they would have been free to return to Castillia and opt to become titled members of society, or/as well as, remain in any land they discovered, owning any wealth acquired after the period of bondage, only making sure to pay half its worth in taxes, preferably gold, to *las católicas majestades* and Don Ruben.

Don Ruben was a wealthy merchant. He was also a financial advisor in the service of *las católicas majestades*. He owned a fleet of trade ships that sailed all the seas of the world, according to Paco. He was well known and well respected in the land, and above all, as Paco recalled, he could be trusted because he had converted to the religion of *las católicas majestades*.

Paco said that at the time when he and Don Jota and the other sixty-six criminals where given another chance to make honest men of themselves, most of Don Ruben's people, in Castillia, were being chastised and chased out, or officially ordered to leave on the pain of death, by *las católicas majestades*. Paco was not sure why Don Ruben's people were being rounded up and expelled by the king and queen of Castillia. He only said it caused less problems and was more peaceful for them, if they simply obeyed the monarchs. But based on what Don Jota told him, and what he heard from people back in the old country, an *Inquistion* was launched by *las católicas majestades* to expel traitors to their god. Paco was still not sure what that meant except that Don Ruben was obedient and became a *converso* himself, so he was safe.

On the day of his departure, Don Jota ordered that all work and activity be stopped in the villages and that every able bodied Taino should get busy loading his ship with gold, maize, tobacco, yuca, cotton, birds, men, women and children. He sent his inspectors to check to make sure, "all the merchandise was securely caged, cased and crated."

As we watched the large ship slowly drift out towards the horizon, getting smaller and smaller, Issi said she felt her heart swelling bigger and bigger. She was standing next to me with her arm around my waist and I could feel every breath she took, in and out. She said she was praying to Guabancex, our goddess of storms, volcanoes and earthquakes. She prayed that the ship be swallowed up by the sea and that Don Jota himself, personally, would be slowly choked, suffocated and drowned by the giant eel, which now possessed the spirit of her own father who loved the sea, and whom Don Jota had condemned to a shameful watery burial.

Sea grapes were in season and Issi let go of me to pick a handful of the purple, round juicy berries. Her ibis tattooed hand froze, and her whole body stiffened, as she clasped her slender fingers around a mellow bunch. I followed her gaze, locked in focus over my shoulder, behind me. I turned around to see Paco approaching.

"No work to do huh, Issi?" he asked, steeling his gaze past me, over my shoulder, hitting Issi. She grabbed the handful of sea grapes, shoved half into my hand and trotted off towards the village.

"Yes sir, I'll get to it right away, sir. See you tonight, Ka…Lilia," she said running off; her words, like her hair, trailing in the wind.

***

By the time I got back to our hut that evening, I had eaten at least four bunches of sea grapes and a half of a whole fresh conch that Paco and I foraged at the beach.

When Issi left, Paco sat with me and we shared grapes and stories until he suggested we take a walk on the beach and a little out to sea where the water reached his elbows and he was not too afraid.

You see, although Paco had travelled to our land on the sea-road, and although he knew how to swim (but not as well as our people), he was still afraid of the sea. He told me that when he was sent away, on the prison ship, as he called it, from Castillia, it was the first time he had ever been on a ship or ever sailed the seas. He said he was so afraid that he cried his way onto the ship, kicking and screaming, with Don Jota screaming at him to shut up and be a man!

Paco said he cried and cried until he passed out and never woke up again until all he could hear was the crash of waves against the space he was curled up in. He called it his bunk, which he said was on the lower deck of the ship, near to the area where they stored extra ropes and weapons. He said, although he had to share the bunk with nine other men, including Don Jota, he was lucky to have got that bunk, since the others were near to the pigs and dogs and horses.

"The noise wouldn't have bothered me so much, you know Loca…it was always noisy anyway, those waves. But the stench though! Unbelievable! The shit and farts and all that!" he said, with a chuckle that sounded sad and a fragile smile fighting not to break out into the frown it really was.

When men didn't grow sick from the filthy conditions on the ship, others died for reasons which Paco said he could not explain.

Six men died.

Two others he said, broke out in huge boils and sores. I never knew what sores and boils were until Paco explained, and it disgusted me. I felt like my insides were trying to leap from my stomach up through my throat, into my mouth.

"Boils ooze out a yellowish greyish viscous liquid. Kinda like the resin you collect from the rubber trees. Mix that with ashes. Then think of crabs that have been dead in the sun for a few days. That's what it smelled like!" explained Paco, trying to contain his own insides.

But as horrific as those images and happenings were, Paco said the one that hit him the hardest was the day, after one whole moon on the seas, when the sentinel climbed the ship's mast to look out for *terra firma*. He said this watchman was about two years older than he was and so they became good friends and would share food and play ball games together, especially when the older men were tired or asleep or drunk on either wine or sea air.

"That day, everyone was so tired and hot and hungry. There was a bit of a breeze, or even wind, I think. I really don't know how to put it, but it felt strange. Like there was a stillness on the seas, but above the clouds it wasn't still. It was a little foggy, so we couldn't really see the top of the mast, but it was still visible somehow. I could have been in a daze, I dunno. This wasn't the first time Mateo was doing this, although he was older, he was lighter than me. Even lighter after a month at sea, I guess…eating the shit we had to eat…. Papa was shouting up at him, 'See anything?' and he would should back, 'Nah!' I told Papa it was useless because of the clouds and that, but he wouldn't listen. He and some other men kept shouting, 'Come on boy, what do you see?' I knew Mateo and I knew he was frustrated and when he's frustrated he just goes quiet."

Paco continued, almost out of breath - it felt like his words were sucking everything out of him. His words were so heavy that sometimes I wished I could help him lift them out.

"They just wouldn't stop shouting. Then there was wind, like a freak gust out of nowhere. It just whooshed through for a brief second then nothing but stillness. Mateo shouted down to us, 'I'm ok, I'm ok!' But before his words reached all ears on deck, six of the men rushed to secure the mast and Mateo too I guess...."

"The men grabbed the mast with such force that all I remember was hearing these echoes of oookkk, hurtling down towards the ship's deck...the mast was still hiding behind these thick and dark folds of fog... Kah! was the last sound I heard... Bones breaking."

Paco spent two and a half moons at sea. He was both elated, as well as emaciated, when the new sentry sounded the alarm, "Land ahoy!" They had finally reached the land of the Indians! They had discovered the rich and flourishing East, at long last! They were beyond jubilant.

They danced and shouted, with what little energy they had, "In-dee-yah! In-dee-yah! In-dee-yah!"

As Paco and I left the white sandy beach and braved it out a little further to sea, we saw some of the pinkest shells littering the shallow sea-floor. One of the huge pink shells housed one of the best tasting conchs I had ever eaten. I suppose now, that anything would have tasted like the best I'd ever had, since I was wrenching with hunger. We ate and splashed and swam and dived and ate and splashed and talked.

Between mouthfuls of clumps of fresh conch, Paco exuded his excitement about his prospects of being finally free and becoming a rich man in both his old and new worlds. He was looking forward to the return of Don Jota who not only promised to bring him the keys to a brighter future, but more importantly, a bride, a wife who looked like him. He said she would be a lady. He smiled and splashed the water, jumping up and down creating white foamy waves atop the crystal clear, turquoise blue, as he jumped. Up. Down.

I was not sure what a lady was, so I asked him.

"Ah Lilia, you will see! Beauty. Class. Just a lady! You won't understand until you see; it's a real pity that there are no ladies around here, but you shall see."

He seemed very pleased and pleased with himself. He took in a gulp of seawater and spewed it in the air, then ducked under the cover of the blanket of the sea to avoid getting wet by the rain he had just created. I laughed and so did he.

***

"Karaya, my child, you are a woman now," whispered my mother.

She and Issi, side by side, led me to the edge of the shallow pool of cool, dark water. I stepped down and in. It felt a little cold at first, then it felt like me.

The moon was full. Its big, round silver face shimmered on the rippled surface of the dark pool I was standing waist-deep in. My mother's brown face glistened in the moonlight. The softness of the light massaged her skin, shine and fragrant with coconut oil. She wore a single petal of red hibiscus, maga, she called it, in her hair and a full garland of golden flowers curled around her neck. Issi was beautifully adorned in the same fashion.

I was naked.

Red hibiscus petals, golden flower petals and blue violet petals floated beside and around me in the pool, in the river, not too far from our hut.

My mother said she was grateful to Atabey, our goddess of fertility, for welcoming me into the sacred realms of womanhood at a time when the overly vigilant Don Jota was away in his faraway land. And a time when the restless Paco was too drunk to care about anything that was happening outside his wine-filled gourd. He only seemed to notice when the gourd threatened to run out of wine, she reflected.

It was just after sunset and I was in a particularly good mood that evening joking and laughing with my mother and Issi whilst we had dinner sitting on the floor of our hut. We were sitting in our *circle* of three, as we did, when suddenly I let out a scream and leapt to my feet, sending my yuca bread and maize flying through the air. My mother and Issi caught such a fright that they too gave flight to the contents of their wooden dinner trays.

"What's the matter, Karaya?" asked my mother.

"Something bit me! I'm going to die!" I was hopping around like a yutia caught in a trap. Terrified. "I'm going to die! Look! Look! I'm bleeding!"

I only stopped skipping and flailing like a freshly hooked marlin when I realised that both women had shifted to a new gear of hysteria. They had both fallen to the floor, bent over with laughter. It was my turn to be shocked, shift to another level of terror. Wide-eyed, frightened and now completely oblivious to my own previously impending death, I asked, "Are you two okay? What's going on? What's so funny?"

Both my mother and Issi, looked up at me, still laughing, tears welling in their eyes, chorused, "You are a woman now, Karaya!"

I did not quite understand what that meant until they told me that now would have been the time, when our men would have taken an interest in me and would have wanted to take me as a wife. Or equally, it was the time I would have also been allowed to look for a man I might have wanted for a husband. It would have been the time I would have been preparing to leave my mother's hut, village or even her land, depending on which man, among our peoples, I had married. But that was that time.

They gently explained the sacred responsibility of womanhood given to us by the great mother, Atabey. They told me that now I would be able to share in the greatest gift of creating and bringing life to the light. I was terrified and fascinated at the same time.

When my mother told me the old, old story of the virgin goddess Atabey who had two sons, and how one son, the great Yucahu became god of the yuca harvest, that sustained our people. I felt very proud to have joined those honoured ranks.

There we all were by the river, performing a fertility ritual in celebration of my womanhood. Issi produced a jar that she had retrieved from its hiding place under a rock by the river. The jar was made from white bone carved in the shape of a woman giving birth. She mixed water with fragrant herbs and poured it on my head. She then stuck a petal of golden flower behind my ear. She took my hand and helped me out of the water, into my mother's awaiting embrace.

On our way back to the hut, my mother was very solemn and pensive. The moon was round and bright and high in the sky. With half of a happy smile, my mother said it reminded her of the night I was born.

When we finally blew out our torches and climbed into our hammocks for the night, my mother cracked the darkness with a gravelly, distant voice.

"Karaya…."

"Yes Bibi."

"Stay away from that Paco."

"…OK Bibi…"

PHASE II

THIS LAND IS YOUR LAND

"Among the natural rights of the colonists are these: first a right to life, secondly a right to liberty and thirdly to property; together with the right to defend them in the best way they can." (Samuel Adams, 1772)[2]

---

[2] Quote from "The Rights of the Colonists" - The Report of the Committee of Correspondence to the Boston Town Meeting, Nov. 20, 1772, by Samuel Adams ("one of the founding fathers of the USA).

***

During the first two moons that Don Jota was away, and Paco took over control, some things changed. Some things seemed different. Nothing particularly transformed, in my eyes anyway, but there was a busyness and heaviness to the place that was not so palpable when Don Jota was around.

One evening whilst I was sitting at the front of our hut skinning the fat iguana that Issi had trapped on the biggest of the ceiba trees that surrounded the plot where we grew peanuts and pineapples, it finally dawned on me.

Men!

Perhaps I had become too busy trying to avoid Paco during the days that I didn't notice the changing scenes of the twilight. I would spend entire days with my mother and Issi, planting yuca or maize or harvesting fruits and berries in the nearby plots. We would be gone for the entire day sometimes. The best days were the hottest. The sun would perform its midday vigil, closely watching our every move, its eyes piercing our naked backs. We would laugh and say the sun seemed to have taken over from Don Jota, but no one really cared. No one feared. In our defiance we would wander to the riverside and plunge our unrobed bodies into the cool, inviting, forbidden waters.

Paco never seemed to miss us. He didn't even bother to question our whereabouts. He was busy rounding up our men, after long days at the gold mines, to have them chop wood and lumber to build his new house, as he called it. This happened every evening just before darkness fell and the miners stopped working for the day, at the mines at least.

Issi said that Paco said that his beautiful wife, whom Don Jota went to fetch in Castillia, deserved to live in a proper house. A wooden house, not some old primitive thatched bohio. Issi had become Paco's chief entertainer after Don Jota left on the ship. Some nights Issi would bid us goodnight and then head straight to Paco's hut, clad only in a robe of darkness. She was following instructions, she said.

Other instructions included sword dances, naked, performed around naked flames incorporating clever or comical contortions, as Don Paco liked. Issi used a piece of stick to mimic the sword skilfully wedged between her feet in the air, as she balanced on her hands and head. I did not find it entertaining or funny. My mother couldn't watch. Issi on the other hand, always grinned maniacally, but her eyes told a different story.

It was always morning when Issi told us about her nocturnal adventures. There was no fire in the hut, and it was not usually dark. Yet there was always a glow, like fire, in her eyes.

She grabbed the sword stick, hunched forward, feet apart, her back moving in wave-like fashion, like the ridges on the back of the iguana I held in my hand. It all seemed and felt a bit creepy. Very much like the silhouettes of the men I had noticed that evening; bent over, weighted down under logs and lumber, for building Paco's house for his beautiful wife. The men, against the grey backdrop of the twilight, resembled the navelless, faceless *hupias* that my mother always told me stories about: the returned spirits of our people who have died.

In all the time I had been alive, I had never seen the face or body of one of our men up close.

One, I was not allowed.

Two, none was lucky enough to get close enough for me to even feel or touch.

Until that day in the maize plot. We heard shrill screams and squeals in the distance, coming from the village square.

I immediately dismissed it as, "Pigs resisting the barbacoa again! How futile!"

"Hush child!" said my mother, interrogating the sounds.

Then Issi, with a sudden burst of loping speed, launched into a sprint in the direction of the squeals. My mother followed. Then I.

The body of a Taino man, blackened by a mix of dried and thick clotted blood, was lying on the path, just a few footsteps from the old ceremonial square, where our people used to play batu. The place where Paco elected to erect his house. No one knew the man's name.

The women who were huddling over his body, crying and wailing, said that he had slipped the night before, carrying logs for construction. His entire head was now in even proportion with his traditionally flattened forehead. Everything was pressed into one flat, featureless face. I wasn't sure if it was the sight or the smell of the corpse that caused me to gag. But I ran aside and vomited.

Before that day, I used to love eating juicy ripe guavas. Since that day I couldn't stand the sight or smell of guavas. They reminded me of the slop, the brains, the blood. Even the seeds reminded me of the crushed teeth, compressed into a one-dimensional, mask-like grin.

Issi was down on her knees next to the body, using her bare hands to scrape all the bits of the man, back together. She moulded his head into human form and pulled his spread-out arms together, folding them across his chest. Some of the other women, still sobbing, helped put him together again, as best as they could. Issi didn't cry.

"We have to move his body. We have to bury him," she whispered to herself as well as to everyone present.

Just as the women started removing their cotton *naguas*, loin cloths, to start wrapping the body to remove it for burial or something, a horse whinnied, and a strange man thundered: "What do you think you're doing? Don't you lazy sluts have work to do?"

"Do we ever not!" retorted Issi. "But we must bury our brother first!"

The other women stood up, cowered, heads bowed, shoulders limp. Issi carried on heaping the remains of the man onto her now bloodied *nagua*.

She jumped to her feet and stiffened as the strange man's whip recoiled from the splat of pain it plastered across Issi's back. Things moved so quickly that the next thing I noticed was Issi grabbing the tail of the whip as it charged towards her face. Block. She wrapped it, once, twice, fast, around her right hand and dragged the tall man off his horse. He fell sideways onto the ground, bruising his right shoulder. He skated on the gravelled floor for a moment then swiftly landed his left boot right between Issi's legs. She shrieked and fell to the floor, clasping the gap between her legs. Her eyes popped open and that daylight flame flickered to life.

All the other women except my mother and me fled back to being busy.

My mother was screaming, "No, no, no!"

The tall strange man, got up, kicked Issi square on the side of her head, picked up his whip and slapped my mother on her left cheek with the handle, "Shut the hell up!" he slammed.

He glared at me, fuming, taking slow, weighted, rocking steps towards me. He wrapped the whip around his right knuckle, rocking, balancing, stepping, right, left, towards me.

"You lucky bastard!" He spat at me, never meaning for it to catch me, but close enough to register his disgust.

"Come now bitches! Move the stinking savage!"

Issi was on her feet again. My mother looked bewildered. I was still a little overwhelmed by all that had taken place.

"What do you mean?" asked my mother.

"You're even dumber than I thought!" he replied, then slowly mouthed the words, one by one.

"I said: move – the – bloody – stinking – savage – over - there!" pointing with his finger.

"So, we can bury him then?" mused Issi.

He turned around, rocked his way back towards Issi and said, "Absolutely not! You have work to do! Enough time wasted already! Feed him to the damned pigs!"

He spat. This time, splat on the man's dead body mounded up in Issi's *nagua*.

My mother, Issi and I, scooped up the remains of our brother. The body was reluctantly heavy. Perhaps as heavy as I had imagined the hefty log that ultimately despatched the poor man. We lumbered our way to the pigs' sty; all the while being watched from behind by the horseman and from above by the sun.

We threw the man into the pigs' sty. The body plopped against the mud and the fat, wobbly creatures grunted with delight. It seemed they were in for a treat of an ample feast. The horseman laughed and brandished his whip. My mother and I scrambled off towards the maize plots, but we had to wait for Issi. She had stopped. She was vomiting.

***

"Which one is it? Where is it? Silly fool! Which one is it?"

I could hear Paco shouting at the top of his lungs amidst the sound of clay jars smashing and baskets of dried maize and yuca being overturned in the storehouse adjoining Don Jota's hut. I did not hear any answers to his questions, but I heard whimpers and suffocated sobs.

"Paco?" I inquired, cautiously entering the barely lit room.

"What the hell is it Lilia? What do you want?"

"Oh nothing, just wondering what's going on here. Perhaps I can help?"

I sauntered closer, closely surveying the obscure room. There was a body curled up in the corner, hands holding her head. I backed up towards her, eyes fixed on Paco. I put my hand on her shoulder and shook her gently. She stiffened and curled herself into an even tighter ball.

"It's ok. You can get up," I said.

She stood up and started speaking, fast and incomprehensible. In my mother's language.

"She's responsible for storage and can't find a damned thing! Useless!" fumed Paco.

He threw an empty straw basket at the woman. We both ducked.

"Leave! Run!" I said, motioning to her. She got the message.

"Now, Paco, what is it you're looking for?" I asked.

"I need that yuca thing."

"Thing?"

"Yes! The poison!"

That thing that Don Jota had forbidden anyone to produce or have in their possession (except himself of course). That thing that our fighters used to poison the tip of their arrows to hunt as well as fight off the Kalinagos whenever they attacked.

I wasn't sure whether Paco was preparing for war. And if he were, I believed the weapons that he and Don Jota and the strange men had, were much more effective than any poisoned arrow. Than any yuca poison.

My mother said that in other villages where the Kalinagos attacked and our men fought back, the arrows were only as effective as the speed and dexterity of their firing and reload capabilities. Kalinagos were swift. Fierce men and women, born and bred for battle.

Even Paco himself knew that. It was Paco who had told me the story of the great battle to the East of Quisqueya, on the island of Boriken when other strange men from Castillia were forced to wipe out the entire Taino population, or most of it.

Paco said our people pretended to be friendly towards the men from Castillia at first, but after one great chief, the friendly Agueybana died (of natural causes Paco would hasten to add), his evil successor (Agueybana II) teamed up in secret, with the Kalingos from the south islands, and tried to overthrow the good

Castillian authorities whose benevolent mission it was to civilise those ungrateful Boriken Tainos.

Given the weaponry of the Castillians: guns, swords, horses, dogs, the Boriken and their Kalinago allies perished woefully – Paco told me with a satisfied grin.

"Chilli dust and poisoned arrows...deliciously primitive. What a joke!"

"Is this a joke?" I asked him, as he kept rummaging through the storehouse.

"Are you going to help me or not? Just leave me the hell alone then, Loca! No time!" he snarled.

"It's stored in a cool dark place, usually" I said. "Ever occurred to you to look where you're standing?"

He kicked the last straw basket out of his way and just as I had suspected, the yuca extract had been hiding in a couple jars underneath a low earth-toned stool that was stooping in the corner. When he finally saw his treasure, the gloomy storehouse cheerfully lit up. He pounced on the jars. Grabbed them. Hugged them to his chest and danced around. I had only ever seen Paco that excited on two occasions. One, the expectation of his beautiful lady wife. Two, when the miners brought him gold.

***

I'd never known Issi to be afraid of anything or anyone. Which was why it struck me as a little odd, the morning when she rushed into our hut like a hurricane flung off course. I was a little shocked. She reeked of vomit and the vomit reeked of guavas and that made me want to throw up too.

Her face was gaunt, and her eyes seemed many days older than they were the day before. She had aged a couple lifetimes. Her eyes looked as though they had seen much more than they ideally wanted.

My mother rolled out of her hammock and rushed to Issi's side.

"You're back early. What happened?" asked my mother.

Issi tried to respond as clearly as she could, through blue and bruised lips; swollen, but not bleeding.

"He hit me! Again!" she blubbered. I drew closer to them joining them on the floor where they were both seated.

"Who? Why?" I asked.

What I didn't know was that Paco had been hitting Issi quite frequently over the past many days and had been complaining that she had got sluggish and lazy and not up to the standard that he expected. "What happened to the firebrand?" he would ask.

That morning she made the grave mistake of throwing up next to him, on his bed. The gagging and vomit spray had woken Paco up and he was not happy about that. He kicked her out of the bed and she landed on her bum, bouncing and sliding in vomit. She retched, and he punched her in her mouth.

"Swallow that, bitch! Get out!"

That was when she came breezing through our hut. A much earlier return than usually expected.

"It seems the herbs haven't worked at all then Issi," said my mother, concerned.

"Not exactly…."

Apparently, it had been a few weeks now that Issi had been having vomiting spells, since the day the pigs ate the remains of that man. My mother had recommended herbal remedies and Issi tried them to no avail. Their prognosis, it seemed, had been way off. Her face wound tight in worry, sitting there next to me on the floor, ageing very fast.

"Tinima, I am pregnant." Silence.

"Been two moons and no blood." Silence.

"I know it misses a moon sometimes, but never two. Now this sickness. I am having his child…."

Those might have well been the hollowest words I had ever heard. Heavy. Deep. Hollow. Echoing through the hut and out beyond time. My mother sobbed and folded herself closer to Issi's and Issi pulled her closer. I just sat there frozen.

My mother and Issi talked for a long while, till the hut started to light up, the sun's reminder that a new day had already been well under way. I didn't hear a word, except the last few my mother uttered, beckoning me to get up and find something to eat before we headed out. I was lost in a daze of numbness. Just like the first day I recalled her uttering those exact words.

"I'll have to have a word with that Paco."

I was filled with the same hollowness that had preceded those very words, on the first occasion, just weeks before.

A woman had come to off-load her concern and suspicion that Paco might have killed three children whom he claimed were a nuisance stealing his papayas that he had fenced off all for himself. My mother was confused and in disbelief. She warned the woman to be careful about spreading such rumours because she herself, and others could also end up dead.

The woman said she knew for sure, because she worked in those same papaya plots and there were a few trees that Paco warned them never to harvest and never to eat from. They could not and did not ask any questions. But she said that Paco said, "Eat it and you'll find out!"

The children used to work gathering rocks for building sites and removing weeds from food plots. They picked fruits and ate them when they saw any. One day Paco spotted them and snapped at the "lazy gluttons" warning them that they would pay for their thieving ways. The woman and the mothers of the children guessed that yuca poisoning might have been responsible for their demise. Their swollen stomachs, darkened eye sockets and bleeding orifices were the obvious signs no one could miss.

My mother and I knew that no one had access to the yuca poison extract, except Don Jota and Paco. I knew for sure that Paco had it in his possession. Tears rolled like time down my mother's face. She struggled to breathe. She held her arms out to the woman, who gently held onto them. As she let go, my mother sighed.

"I'll have to have a word with that Paco."

***

"Ship! Ship!"

The announcement rung throughout the village, passing from man to mouth like a bird call in mating season. Horsemen, dogs and everyone else bolted towards the shore.

"Ship! Ship!" the shouts continued, echoing strained strains of celebration.

Don Jota had returned. It seemed.

Canoes and small boats rowed out to sea. Offloaded cargo. Then back to land. More strange men. More guns. More pigs. More dogs. Yams. Beans. Chickens. Cows. Lemon and orange plants. Banana plants. And a priest. All present.

Don Jota, absent. Beautiful lady wife for Paco, also a no show.

People were frightened of the newly introduced, relatively large, colourfully feathered, flightless birds called chickens. They fluttered around in joyful bewilderment and made ugly noises. I could not think of any other bird on Quisqeya that made such an annoying racket. The larger male birds were inappropriately raucous. They were chief disruptors of sleep. They could be counted on, early every morning, to wake up the whole village with their loud endless cackle. They did not sing, like normal birds. They crowed. I hated them.

The cows were another nuisance. They could have well been the most sluggish animals ever created. They chewed constantly, even when they were not chewing on anything. They made loud noises too. Even louder than the big male chickens. We did not like them much. They trampled everything and ate everything. I used to think that pigs were annoying, but generally they were kept away from everyone and only made grunting sounds. They liked mud and dirt and they ate any and everything - but at least they weren't so noisy, compared to the others whose core distinction was to broadcast their existence to the very limits of village! Pigs did not require much work or care either. But these cows!

Horses and dogs were not really our concern. The strange men looked after these themselves and generally took very good care of them, like they weren't really animals, but friends, or even family. They certainly received better treatment than that meted out to our people, to be fair.

These new animals were farm animals, Paco said. The type Don Jota had told me about some time ago. He had grown up with them, he had told me then.

Now many things had started to make sense. This whole idea of farming made sense, but I did not like it. These silly animals needed to be looked after and these new plants, bananas, beans, oranges, needed to be tended. Some men, but mostly women, were given full responsibility of taking care of these new additions to the village. "Care for them like your own children; don't let them die!" Paco and his new best friend, Don Andres Cervantes, admonished the new farmers.

It was Don Cervantes who had taken control of the ship, he said, after Don Jota died at sea on his return voyage, just six days before they arrived back in Quisqueya.

Don Jota had taken ill and had stopped eating for nearly thirteen days. He had broken out in boils and sores. The way Don Cervantes described it, it was as if a pestilence of niguas had laid eggs all over his body, especially his nether regions, and all the eggs matured and popped at the same time. Don Jota had degenerated into a soggy log of smelly, blueish, greenish slime leading up to the time of his death. No one could touch him, or even dared. He was kept above deck under a waterproof canvass. And with the last test-prod from a long metal pole, for proof of life, or not, it was confirmed that he had exited this realm. That same metal pole was used to push his slimy remains overboard, to a watery end.

Issi thanked the goddess Guabancex for hearing her prayer. Don Jota would finally face her father in a final stand-off in the life beyond the bosom of the sea. She prayed again that her father would show Don Jota no mercy after his final demise. She hoped he would be banished to a restless unending fall to into the dark, cavernous, abyss of the sea.

My mother and I were indifferent.

Paco on the other hand, was visibly upset by the news. He kept to himself for days. Drinking maize wine and a lot of the sherry that Don Cervantes had gifted him, on caution to slowly sip and savour. Paco guzzled and swigged.

***

Padre Juan Perez was the priest who arrived with the last ships. Padre Perez, was a rotund, heavy-set man who wore long flowing brown or black robes, loosely tied around the waist with fatly woven brown cotton threads. He wore an amulet around his neck. He called it a cross. He walked and spoke ever so slowly. We sometimes wondered whether it was the weight of his words or the weight of his huge, protruding stomach that made his words and gait slow to such a halting, cumbersome glide. He would always whisper breathy blends of inaudible words and then reach for his amulet, kiss it and wave it in the air, gazing up at the sky. Issi said that he must be talking to his ancestors or perhaps he was not in his right mind. He called everyone his child and that confused everyone. He had no wife and no family, yet he considered us his children. That made us generally agree with Issi's conclusion. This priest was a mad man.

My mother did not like him. When he first met my mother, he palmed her head and closed his eyes and waved his amulet. He touched the amulet on her stubbed arms and her forehead. When he opened his eyes, my mother staring coldly and frightfully into his green eyes, he whispered, "Bless you my child! The very epitome of his suffering."

He had taken to calling my mother, Amarga, and that incensed her even more. She had no idea what that name meant, and the priest didn't bother to ask whether she had already had a name, herself. He took a shine to my mother and would have her walk with him daily as he went about his business of saving the innocents – his name for our people.

My mother used to return to our hut in the evenings, angry and fuming after every day spent with Padre Perez. She said he had an odd fascination with her arms and sometimes would ask her to stand in the sun and hold her arms outstretched. He would kneel in her shadow, murmuring his whispers and tossing kisses to the sky. After his ritual he would ask her to lead him to meet other villagers and their children especially. He took the children and babies in his arms, kissed their foreheads and rubbed his finger over their rounded mounds, muttering, "Thank you blessed mother for saving this innocent savage."

Padre Perez decided that everyone must start attending what he called Mass. Mass was held in the former ceremonial square. He lamented the absence of a building where Mass should ideally be held. He explained that Mass required a respectful and noble gathering place, just like the ones they had back in Castillia. This place, after all, was where his god had his dwelling. And just like a miracle from providence, he said, the good lord had provided, Paco's newly built house. With no beautiful lady wife to occupy Paco's house, Padre Perez had a place for Mass, a place where his god could respectably dwell. His very own church, as he called it. And with no Don Jota to move back into Don Jota's large hut, Paco could remain and fill his father's shoes.

The masses flocked to Mass on the first day of every week. Padre Perez had a white cotton robe made for my mother. She had to wear it to Mass or on special occasions designated by him. And she had to always stand next to, or behind Padre Perez.

When Issi's eyes caught my mother's, at the first Mass, they both broke out into hysterical fits of giggles. Padre was in the middle of his passionate sermon about the holy virgin mother when, his train of thought derailed into chaos, amidst the giggles. He flung himself around to investigate the source of such irreverent hilarity. His large belly and long flowing gown slowly followed the brisk turn of his neck and head, almost in tandem but not simultaneously. Poor Padre Perez lost his balance and toppled over. My mother tried to catch him, but she couldn't. Even if she wanted to, she had no hands. The giggles rose into a crescendo of cacophonous laughter that filled Paco's house, turned house of god. Cackles, like those chickens, rose to high heaven.

Padre Perez completed two full rolls on the floor, rumbling and tumbling like the barrels that came on the ships. He slowly quickly got up off the floor. He regained a kind of disoriented composure, waving his amulet, his flabby arm jowls sagging as he waved.

He kissed the amulet, cleared his throat and asked, "Where was I my children? What was I saying?"

Issi raised her hand.

"Yes, my child," encouraged Padre Perez, "please stand up and tell us, my child."

Issi stood up. Cleared her throat and began:

"You were telling us about the holy virgin mother who had a son, who you say is our saviour."

Padre seemed very pleased. He nodded and said, "Thank you, my dear child," but Issi wasn't finished.

"Yes Padre," she continued, "but you forgot that the holy virgin mother Atabey, had not only one son, but two. Twins actually: Yúcahu and Guacar. It was Yucahu

100

who became our saviour and gave us the wholesome yuca to sustain us. And then, his twin brother, Guacar, became envious of Yucahu, forever trying to destroy everything Yucahu created."

With that Issi took her seat, wearing a cunning smile disguised by a transparent veil of neutrality.

Everyone was looking at Issi and nodding. The priest did not look so pleased. He snapped, "Stop that heretic talk right now! No more of this heresy! That kind of blasphemy shall never fall from your lips again. Ever! Enough! Purge those silly…erm, myths…and fantasies from your simple minds and I shall set you free… with the truth. The truth of the one true virgin mother and her only…, well not her only…, but the only one son that can save us, including you blessed, innocent creatures!"

Everyone was still looking around. Confusion inked a jagged tattoo over all their faces. Padre Perez, waved his amulet, kissed it and breathlessly burbled, "You are dismissed! Go in peace! Just go!"

***

Since the day the ship arrived, bearing no wife and no father for him, Paco hardly had any peace. I knew he wasn't sleeping well or sleeping at all, on some nights. His endless parade of nocturnal entertainers failed to neither satisfy nor tire him out enough to fall asleep. Issi commented that he had grown detached and disinterested in whatever the goings-on were and had become more interested in a more sordid type of voyeurism. He would enlist the newly arrived talents of his fellowmen, especially his amigo and adviser, Don Andres, to perform their best shows of manhood and masculinity, with a pick of any of the women in attendance.

I was not sure, when I saw him, going about my chores, whether he was simply exhausted or whether he had aged a great deal since the last time I saw him up close. His call out to get my attention sounded weary and long. Like a day without sun.

"Loca! Come here! Where have you been hiding?" He asked, crooking his neck, lifting his head to peer between his legs.

He was lying under a broad-leafed tree, shading out the midday sun; on his back with his thighs raised, legs sprawled at an angle.

"You know how it is around here, Paco," I smiled and drew close to where he was, "a lot to do, especially all this harvesting."

I laid down my basket and squatted next to him. He arched his body enough to stretch his right arm out enough to give my head a rub.

"Well, you know Loca, if it ever gets too much for you, there are others here to do the work. That's why they're there! Don't you forget that. Just don't do too much, ok?" He smiled at me and flattened out again.

"I'll be sure not to forget."

Next to him, near his head, Paco had a small pile of papers. I had only seen paper when Don Jota used to say he was making plans to turn the village into civilised town and the other time when he was looking at maps, preparing to go back to his land. Don Jota used to write things down in large books, but I could not read them. We didn't know how to read. My mother said that Padre Perez said that part of his mission was to teach special ones among us to read and write like them. My mother did not ask what qualified as special, she only said she supposed we would have soon found out.

The church, Paco's house of god, was now complete. Complete with a giant wooden amulet, like the one Padre Perez wore around his neck, hoisted in front. It had rows of seats made from bamboo and wood, so that we could sit more comfortably when Padre held his Mass. Padre said that comfort was essential to learning about his god. Comfort prevented distraction, he said. Issi said we were going to need much more than comfort, to stop us laughing or falling asleep listening to the hog shit that Padre was trying to make us digest. She was usually unfettered by nonsense, but she sounded really rankled when she added, "He irks me! That barren barrel of a man, shuffling around like a lost hupia, speaking in shh-shhs like cows pissing. Someone ought to really check if he actually has a navel!"

"So, what's that?" I asked, pointing at Paco's papers.

"Oh that…" Paco began.

"A letter from Papa."

He sighed, looking weary. There were dark wrinkly circles around his eyes.

"Padre Perez delivered it to me. He said that Papa had written it couple weeks before he died, you know, just in case."

My mind wandered then, considering what it must have felt like for Don Jota to know he was dying. I knew we all had to die, but I wondered whether he was afraid or somehow boldly ready and prepared to confront this destiny. I guess what concerned me the most in that moment, was that I had no idea what Don Jota believed or thought about death, dying, the after-life, ancestors. What if Issi were right? Was Don Jota worried about the final face off with her father? And I suppose many others he had been a little more that cruel towards, this side of the abyss.

I wondered where his spirit went. Had it gone anywhere even? Our people, when we died, our spirits transitioned to Coaybay, on the other side of the sunset.

"Do you want me to read it to you?" asked Paco, nudging me back to his realm.

"Erm, yes. Sure. Why not?"

Don Jota wrote:

"*Dear Paquito,*

I think it wise to start putting *pluma* to paper as this voyage back to you and that beautiful land we claimed in the name of our great king and queen, might not actually materialise for me. We are still sailing, still weeks away before reaching land.

Lying here in my bunk, listening to the waves crash against this beast of a ship, hearing the ruckus the animals, both two and four legged, are making, puts me in mind of you and your first and hopefully last voyage across this vast ocean. I remember how terrified you were. How every unexpected gust, and every violent sway of the ship, made you panic…so much that I sometimes thought, then, that I might lose my boy on this vicious but hopeful adventure. I hoped and prayed then, that you would hold on till we reached the promised Indies, wherever they were hiding. I was happy when we finally spotted land and had the chance at a new and fruitful life.

As I write, and I try to every day, I feel my body rebelling against my every will and wish for it to move or do anything at all. The only thing growing these days, is the pain I feel coursing throughout my entire being. I write a few lines at a time, then my fingers lose the will to grasp even the lightest *pluma*. I think I might have to ask Padre Perez to be my scribe at some point, if things get any worse. I have also had a quiet word with the Padre to offer me absolution when the time comes, so not to worry. I imagine I shall be ok with the one up yonder.

The fact that you are even reading this letter, means that I did not make it back. And I shall try to explain why. There is no doctor to give treatment or diagnosis, so I have to go with what I know, or think I know.

You see, being back in the old country was bittersweet. I was happy to finally go back and make amends for the mercy we, you and I had been granted. I was happy to be able show off all the gold and exotic plants and foods and people. I was happy for a chance to be truly free again, and to live and enjoy my wealth and prestige as a noble *conquistador* that brought civilisation to these primitive corners of the earth, in the name of *las católicas majestades*.

I looked forward to seeing that Don Ruben. I wanted to show him what excellent returns I had made on his wise investment. I had even hoped that perhaps he could arrange an audience with the king and queen, him being their trusted advisor and all that.

We arrived back in the Port of Cadiz and once the cargo had been accounted for, I thought that perhaps I should try to have a bit of fun before getting down to business the following day. I must say though, that the natives I brought with me were such a hit with the merchants and aristocrats! Who would have thought?

The women and girls fetched a good price and the men did ok as well, considering how useless they really are. Some trader from Toledo took about three of the savages, apparently to perform as acts in his travelling circus. He wanted breeding pairs, but he could only have three since we had to take the best of the lot to show to their majesties.

Anyway, I told the trader that he had made a good investment and I advised him to try to have them breed as soon as possible because his best return will be on the younglings. They won't be as silly and corrupted as the older ones and they would be less likely to want to throw themselves from high places or hang themselves or starve themselves to death, as you know they are prone to do. It's as if they get some satisfaction from such savagery.

I warned the *tipo* from Toledo that these savages loved death and have no fear of it, so he would be wise to watch and control their every move, if he didn't wish to waste his money, after all.

But I digress.

I wanted to have a little fun, as I was saying. I wanted to taste and feel the folds of real women again. It had been so long, you see. I went to a brothel near the ship yard, in the town. It was nicely lit place in the basement of a tavern, much like the place where Angustia, your mother, worked. Well, not in the brothel, but you know what I mean. But then again, it might well have been. I had some flashbacks when I first happened upon the place, but I tried to banish any thought of that past and that wretched tavern.

I went in, had some drinks, talked to the boys about my adventures and exploits and they glowed green with envy. You should have seen their ugly faces! I had money, so I paid for drinks for all of them and then went to the basement to have the fun I had been missing and longed to make up for!

Lying here, looking back, feeling as terrible as death, I reckon I was missing much more than I had initially had in mind. Seems the fucking wenches gave me the gift of the clap or something. Something that's making me break out in sores. Something that's causing me to piss, shit and sometimes vomit blood and blue.

Blue! I don't know what it is but it smells foul and makes me not want to eat anything.

I have got sores all over my body and I can't even sit for long. I can't stand either. The blasted boils are even under my feet. The best thing, the only thing really, I can do, is lie down. I feel like a slug. No one wants to touch me. Can I blame them? Lying down is a pain, don't get me wrong, but once I'm plastered in this slush of pain, I think my brain forgets about it. The only thing worse than the stench and boils and sores, is the itching. It itches, and I can't even scratch. Well, I can. If I want to rip off lumps of my own decaying flesh, of course. I am dying slowly, painfully, right before my own blinking eyes!

So, business.

After that night in the tavern, satisfied as a sailor, I went to look for Don Ruben. The clerk told me to wait. And I waited. Long. Then some *diputado* from the court of their majesties came to fetch me and took me to an old office near the centre of town. There I met with two old be-wigged, bespectacled, nictitating, fat bastards wearing thick black robes. I honestly believe scales would have been more befitting garments, to match their cold-blooded reptilian manners!

Short of the matter is that our deal was off. The two lumps of men, crouched over a huge wooden desk, hands clasped, and like a somewhat over-rehearsed duet, they croaked:

'Well, you see son, due to current the atmosphere in Castillia, these days, you understand, their majesties deem it fit to cancel any previous contracts made by, uhhh, one who has been found to commit treason, uhhh, in the eyes of holy law, no less….'

'Treason? Who?'

'Uhhh, do allow us to finish, son…gracias.'

I sat there feeling dazed, weighted and dead as a stone. Didn't hear another word. Just saw their beaks moving, mouthing tautologous litanies of useless platitudes.

'So, son, uhhh, by royal decree, the ships and all other assets foreign and domestic, are now property of the crown. Uhhh, Ruben del Soto, persona non-grata, uhhh, you see, had to be relinquished of his rights to citizenship, uhhh, for harbouring traitors of his kind,' the dim duo sputtered on.

I couldn't hold it in any longer, so I asked, 'Where, pray tell, is Don Ruben…?'

Four cloudy cataract eyes darted at me, over the rims of spectacles held in place by rubbery rounded noses. The eyes hurled chilling warnings conveyed by words meant to remind me of my place.

'That's none of your concern…uhhh, son! All you need to know is that, uhhh, for his crimes, the crown confiscated all that belonged to Del Soto. Ships included. All contracts null and void.'

Still in a daze, I might have imagined it, but I could swear the two tongues slithering out from the holes in their faces had two tails each, split down the middle!

Anyway, I composed myself and whispered an apology. To which the two chorused, "I think we are, uhhh, done here, son. *Señor De los Lobos*! Their majesties are eternally grateful for your service."

Then one motioned to the *diputado*, "Please see him out."

The other handed me my new commission papers. And again, the two, in one voice, wished me, "Bon Voyage!"

My son, we lost our freedom. Again. We lost our promised wealth and all that we have slaved for.

I should mention here, by the way, that with news of that loss, we lost your beautiful bride to be: Doña Flor-Alba Corredor.

News travelled fast regarding these new and latest developments, especially given that they were backed by royal decree. Flor-Alba's father considered that the new state of affairs would be of no benefit to his honour or his daughter's future wellbeing. He claimed he would not be a willing participant to his daughter's sentence to a life of servitude and savagery on the wild side of the world. He lost faith and trust in my promise.

I sorely apologise, Paquito. I would advise that you also make other arrangements in the situation and circumstances you find yourself. I know you have been enjoying yourself as a young man. Keep doing so. But find one, the better among them, and make her your one. I would not hasten to call whatever you decide upon, marriage. Marriage is for civilised folks. Until such time, if such a time ever comes, keep having fun, but make one yours still. You will need it. Just like my very own Tinima. You should look after her and Lilia.

Just to pick up, I left the office rattled and in a state of complete shock, to be quite honest. They sent me off with an empty thank you and a single note ordering and detailing my next passage and voyage to the Indies in continued humble and faithful service *to las católicas majestades*.

I wandered about the streets for a bit, can't remember if it was for a long or short time. I was happy to have eventually found a tavern to drown this dragon of fiery sorrows that had now beset me. I lost the will and credentials to boast so I talked to the other men sitting around, dearly and stubbornly clinging to some semblance of a will to simply breathe, in the hope of some kind of tomorrow.

It seemed Don Ruben had gained a wealth of infamy for himself, in the time we have been gone. Some people were saying that he had committed heresy and was dismissed wearing a badge of shame. They believed he had fled to Portugal or to Morocco, following throngs of his people who had failed to live up to the call to be faithful, to "convert or die". People believed Don Ruben and his people were mere imposters trying to save their own skins, and not true believers in the holy faith of *las católicas majestades.*

The men in the tavern had a different tale to tell.

Apparently, Don Ruben had provided refuge for a man and his wife, who had been banished from Andalusia. The word was that said man and wife were *conversos* who had failed to honestly declare all their wealth and riches. They sold an entire vineyard and a stable full of horses to *las católicas majestades*, in return for one full sack of grain! That right there, I must say, was a true example of holy and righteous desperation! "Convert or die!" right?

But I won't be so quick to lavish praise, though. The infidels were clearly intent on continuing their cunning tricks. When the shack they were left with to live in was searched by the Inquisitors, on another occasion, a bag containing thirty pieces of silver was found. Undeclared. Can you believe these dishonest bastards!

That was obviously a direct affront to the royal decrees of *las católicas majestades* and a heretic and blasphemous undermining of the holy faith. The man and wife from Andalusia were sent packing again. This time on the pain of death.

The *conversos* managed somehow, to miraculously find room and refuge at Don Ruben's inn. Not for long though. True to form, to save her own skin, Don Ruben's own housemaid, one of his own kind, ratted him out. But you know Paquito, am I surprised? They would willingly denounce anything and anyone to secure a place at the table. Even if it is hog that is being served!

Don Ruben's servant sent word out, that Don Ruben, servant to the crown, had been harbouring fugitives and plotting the assassination of Inquistors.

The men in the tavern said that that was the end of it really. Mob justice took over and righteous Castillians rallied to revoke Don Ruben's, and the others like him, citizenship and right to exist in Castillia. It has not been officially reported, recorded or acknowledged, but the streets have it that the heretics were burnt at the stake, in an ultimate "auto-da-fe".

I have not eaten for a few days now and strength has all but failed me. What little I have left, I shall use to wish you well my son.

That land we so faithfully claimed, Quisqeya, is now rightfully your land. Claim it my son! Make it bend to your will. Just as our people would do anything to protect the sacrosanctity of Castillia, so should you do whatever it takes to build your new land. Build your life. You are now home. Make it home. Make it whatever you want it to be and whomsoever stands in your way, bid them, like a true Castillian, 'convert or die!'

Tu Papa.

Juaquin De los Lobos"

When Paco finished reading the letter, I cushioned him the warmest embrace and allowed him to finish his sobbing on my shoulders. On hearing Don Jota's last words, I had very many questions. Questions for which Paco might have had the answers but that moment was not the time to be asking questions, of him, at any rate.

"What am I to do now?" sighed Paco, lifting his head from my shoulders, looking directly into my eyes, as if for the very first time.

***

Nearly a moon had gone by since Issi's announcement that she was carrying Paco's spawn. In a twisted way, that child would also happen to be both my niece or nephew and my cousin.

Issi seemed to have resignedly accepted her fate. She kept swelling and glowing as she went about her daily business. Some nights she would disappear, even when not summoned to carry out her nocturnal entertainment duties. She would return just before dawn, just after those loud silly flightless birds began to crow, announcing the dawn of a new day. She was always wet and covered in soot. Her whole body as black as her hair. She wore traditional garments, covering only her breasts and lower parts. She always seemed happier with every return and would make up new ballads in her language. She sung loud. Even defiant:

> *"The water breaks like morning dew*
>
> *No rain or showers here*
>
> *All serene, in lower case.*
>
> *Hope takes the name I'll never forget*
>
> *Faith begs to do the same.*
>
> *Souls march on in full circle, not lost or bound in chains*
>
> *Just one by one surrendering to life's great roll of names!"*

I tried to read my mother's knowing, deadpan gaze as she busied herself with morning chores. My mother hummed under her breath. She had a unique skill that she mastered to perfection. She could stare at someone but also manage to ignore them, all at the same time. The suspense became too much for me, so I blurted out, "Okay, okay! Can someone fill me in here? What am I missing?"

"Ah nothing!" sung Issi.

"Yeah, nothing indeed," said my mother.

"Issi, you might want to shut up and tell Karaya what's got into you lately...apart from the obvious, of course."

Issi stopped singing.

She started to make long, exaggerated, rhythmic, strides towards my hammock. Like a dance. Grinning ear to ear. Head moving side to side with each step. Eyes wide open and bright like the sun, which incidentally had already started to seep in through the thatch of our hut.

"Welllll...," she rattled, rolling the words off her tongue, to a beat, "I have a plllllaaannn, plan!"

"Okay Issi, I got the song and dance, enough now! Just tell me what's going on! Should I be worried or happy? Right now, I'm confused! Just tell me!"

"Wow, alright then! So serious! Nothing to be worried about, first of all. Second, yeah, you should be happy. What else is there to be? This whole joke of a place and life... Anyway, happy, is what I was saying."

"Happy…and…"

She made her way to my hammock, holding on to the side, shedding traces of her blackness all over it.

"Remember Ayanti, we always talked about…? Killed the buggers and disappeared like a hupia at daybreak?"

"Yeah. What about her, then? Isn't she supposed to be dead or something?"

"Hmmm, more something. Definitely not dead…if she can in fact die, who knows…?"

"Issi. The point?! Story after sunset please!"

122

"Tinima, can you hurry up and get this child something down her stomach! Wow! Cross this morning, are we!"

I raised myself from the hammock and hung my feet over the sides, facing Issi. I smiled to myself as she continued her story. It was almost comical watching her blinking eyes, pearly teeth and red tongue flicker, shutter and appear now and again, against the backdrop of blackness, with every word, every smile, every grimace.

"Well, as I was trying to say, Ayanti is alive and I've been meeting up with her…and some others."

***

The day finally came when my mother managed to have that talk with Paco. She was doing the usual rounds with Padre Perez, dressed in her ceremonial robe and using every opportunity to cast a holy shadow in the sun, to the utter delight of the priest.

Padre Perez, Paco and some others of their men were gathered around the old ceremonial square, turned site of Paco's house, turned church. The church did in fact become Paco's church in a sense, as Padre Perez suggested that they name the church after Paco. It was then I understood, after all this time, that in Paco's language, his real name was Francisco. I found it curious. I began to ponder the true meaning of a name. I thought about my own name, names even. And that told enough of a story in itself.

The men had taken a break from drawing up plans on big pieces of paper and from naming Paco's house: *La iglesia de San Francisco*. Paco was still beaming with his sense of achievement and accomplishment when my mother asked him for a moment of his time. They went inside *la iglesia de San Francisco* and took a seat at the back, which was confusing, because in truth, it was the front, since that was where people were meant to enter from.

"Thank you, Don Paco, for your time. I know it must be hard for you…um, with Don Joaquin, um…"

"Great, Tinima, great, but is there anything else you called me away for? Something important perhaps?"

"Oh sorry, Don Paco, yes, sure. It's Issi, you see…"

"What about Issi…?"

"Well, you see, she hasn't been very well lately, and I was uh, wondering whether you could, you know, give her some time off, uh, at nights, Don Paco."

"What the hell are you saying? Telling me what to do?"

"No, no, not at all Don Paco…uh…"

"Stop interrupting me! Who do you think you are, trying to tell me how to live?! You think I'm Papa. How dare you talk to me like that!"

Paco jumped to his feet, towering over my mother, shouting and stomping. Words echoing and feet like drumbeats reverberating through the hollow, made-for-acoustics, hallowed chamber of *la iglesia de San Francisco*.

My mother sprung to her feet. Arms waving. The loose and droopy sleeves of the big white gown motioning like giant seagulls caught in a gale.

"Well, Paco!" gnarled my mother, "Joaquin left you big boots to fill! Looks to me like you're stumbling! You have no heart! At least Joaquin listened!"

A swift and sturdy slap connected Paco's sprawled and calloused right palm to my mother's left jaw. The slap echoed throughout the hallowed hollow. My mother spat blood. Into Paco's face. Another slap. And another. And others, even.

My mother collapsed to the floor looking up at Paco, towering over her, in his church. He spat at her.

The slimy goo landed right between her eyes, gliding in glistening viscosity towards the inner corner of each eye, making up for the tears that never seemed to come.

"I am not my father, I'd have you know, bitch! And if it weren't for Lilia, I have the mind to finish the work my father started and chop off the rest of your stumpy arms, then beat you with them till…! That's what you deserve…talking to me like that…."

He planted one more firm kick to her abdomen and only set off to leave, when the whoosh of shuffling feet edged towards them. It was Padre Perez.

"Oh, Dios mio! What happened here Amarga, my child?"

He helped my mother back to her feet. She spat out some more blood and used the huge sleeves, of the now blemished white gown, to wipe Paco's phlegm from her eyes.

"Nothing Padre, just a misunderstanding between the Don Paco and me. Let's carry on with your visits, Padre."

***

From that day on, Paco seemed determined to march forward in his own strides. No one dared mistake his steps for stumbles potentially brought on by his wearing Don Jota's old, ill-fitting boots. Whatever, in his estimation, was positioned left, he would put to right, on his own terms. He was a man living in the light of the midday sun. No shade or shadow of the father could eclipse his splendour. He became Don Francisco de los Lobos. His own man, in his own land. And everyone who never knew, would soon know.

One day one of the miners collapsed from exhaustion. This was nothing new, but Paco's punishment was new. The gold mines were located on the rocky side of one of the mountains that stood as guardians over our land. Waterfalls and streams flowing from the face of the cliffs were like crystal tears of joy giving life to everything and everyone that lived below, in the valleys and surroundings. Huge birds like hawks and eagles and vultures nested and soared way up in the craggy loveliness of the mountain. The view, many said, simply took your breath away. On some days, when the wind was mild and as soft as whispers, one might have even forgotten to breathe – taking in the beauty of it all.

It was on one such day that Paco took the exhausted miner and told him to, "get off your knees weakling and jump!" The man resisted and begged for his life, promising to work harder and to never collapse again. All that pleading fell on deaf ears.

Paco, in those days, only listened to Paco. He marched over to the edge of the cliff, near the mouth of the mining cave, told the miner to stop wasting his time: "fly away then, if you can't jump!"

Paco sauntered closer and closer to the miner, extended his booted leg and with a slight push, like an exhale, sent the miner flying. There was no sound, except for the swoosh of wind that enveloped the miner delivering him to a flinty bluff some distance below. The jagged platform of hard rock jutted out to receive its delivery of splattered guts and brain. Paco peeked over the cliff edge, then stepped back to maintain his balance as he howled out the most satisfyingly sadistic laugh.

On another occasion, a young woman was caught bathing in the river just beyond the bushes of the guava plots. Padre Perez and my mother were out on their usual missions checking in on all of Padre's many children. The village huts were not far from the plots, so it was usually easy to fetch water for food plots or for use in our huts.

On that particular day, my mother said she heard loud screams coming from beyond the bushes, in the direction of the river. Padre Perez grabbed her arm and they both fumbled through the bushes until they happened upon one of Paco's men, holding one of our women.

He had held her around her waist, hoisted under one arm, horizontal, feet off the ground. She was naked. She was kicking and screaming and biting the man who held her like a sack of maize.

"Put me down! Let me go!" she screamed and struggled.

"Come, come, my children, what's the matter here, now?" pleaded Padre Perez.

"I just caught this one bathing naked in the river! That's against the rules! She should be punished!" said the man, enraged and out of breath.

"Bloody bastard bit me! Owww!"

He dropped her and gripped his side, his face scowling with a putrid mixture of pain and anger.

The girl got up and as she tried to bolt off to safety, still screaming, the single bang of a bullet escaping a gun, silenced her screams and stilled her strides. She careened forward as the bullet hit her, smack in the back of her head. Her naked body, swaddled in blankets of dust, laid sprawled out face down in the dirt.

Blood dribbled out of the hole in her head in lazy, gulpy spouts, adding a dark red sheen to the already dank strands of black lifeless hair.

"Oh, Dios mio!" said Padre Perez.

My mother was in shock and so was the man who had previously tried to punish the kicking, screaming, biting girl who now laid lifeless on the ground.

Everything happened so quickly leaving everyone baffled as to what had actually happened to the young woman. Until the sound of hooves, strutting into a canter, resolved the mystery. They turned their heads, only to see Paco riding away, astride Don Jota's old stallion, tucking away his musket.

PHASE III

THIS LAND IS MY LAND

"Let them look to the past, but let them also look to the future; let them look to the land of their ancestors, but let them look also to the land of their children."
(Wilfrid Laurier, 1905)[3]

---

[3] From speech at Inauguration of Province of Alberta, by Wilfrid Laurier, 7th Prime Minister of Canada (11 July 1896 – 6 October 1911), "Let Them Become Canadians," September 1, 1905.

***

Ayanti, to me, for a long time, remained a figment of fantasy. Issi's stories of their clandestine encounters in the caves under the shroud of darkness, masked in sooty blackness, remained sources of great intrigue to me.

Ayanti and others, Cacique Enriquillo among them, were plotting to reclaim our village and the land from Paco and his men.

A strange bird, as Issi recounted, lured her from the guava plots to the edge of a nearby hill. Beneath the hill hid the darkest caves. The caves were not easily visible from the hill above or from the sea below. The caverns stooped behind a wall of waves which crashed violently against rigid columns of black ironshore. I remember Don Jota once referring to them as rough, sharp, rock formations – to be avoided at all costs.

Ayanti and Cacique Enriquillo did not avoid them. They knew the caves, the waves and the rocks. And as the ironshore and caves had shielded and protected our people, it was time for them, they believed, to reclaim and protect the land.

Issi said the colourful bird, which as far as she knew, only inhabited the farthest end of our land, landed on a shrub near to where she was working in the field. The bird, she said, did everything to get her attention, preening its feathers, fluttering about a little, then taking flight, then diving back onto the shrubs, preening, then flying circles around her, then darting off towards the coast, then back again. Repeat.

Issi dropped her digging stick and followed the bird after its third dramatic rendition of its solo act. The bird flew just beyond the edge of the hill, then hovered over the rough, sharp, rock formations that stood in defiance of the vicious waves.

Being Issi, she scurried downhill, braved the battering waters and flung herself, curled into a ball, head-first into the abyss of darkness.

"To be honest, I really thought I was dead or something. Because I don't even remember swimming. Thing is I don't remember breathing either, or even struggling to. It's like there was no need to," reminisced Issi.

"Hahaha! So, you haven't lost it all, have you, Issi?" said the voice of darkness, placing a firm hand on her shoulder.

She was not puzzled or afraid. She instantly recognised the voice as Ayanti's. Issi thought perhaps she had been taken to the home of the ancestors, somewhere beyond the belly of the sea.

"Ayanti?!"

"Yes, my dear child. I am right here."

Issi turned around in the dark to face the direction of the voice of darkness. She saw nothing. No face. No body. Just a pair of eyes: gold, like maize, piercing the surrounding husks of darkness.

"Light!" said a voice, coming from a little distance inside the underground haven. It was the powerful voice of Cacique Enriquillo.

Almost immediately, following the sound of leaves rustling and stones rubbing against each other, a streak of sunlight streamed through a hole in the roof of the cave. Mabo, a slender, muscular man, was holding a long stick which reached up to the roof of the cave, burrowing its way outside, exposing a hole just big enough to allow the inflow of just enough light, from outside.

Ayanti introduced her entourage.

Cacique Enriquillo. Mabo. Caguax. Niti.

They were all covered in a pasty soot that glistened in the dark as the light bounced off their bodies.

Ayanti looked down at Issi's rounded belly, then glanced back up to meet her eyes. There was a sadness there that both women felt and shared. She took Issi's hand as Cacique Enriquillo motioned everyone to sit, in a circle, on the wet gravelly floor of the cave. The waves crashing on the outside became the perfect backdrop for what was to follow. The sounds from the outside created a certain rhythm that kept in sync with each word spoken, and each breath taken, individually and collectively, as one.

Courtney J. Scott

"So, my brothers and sister, this is Issi whom I always spoke about!" said Ayanti, giving Issi's hand a gentle squeeze as she introduced her to the group.

"I think it's clear that despite all she and our people have been going through, she's still good for the fight! She's a tough one. In tune with the ancestors and will definitely help our cause to bring us all home."

Everyone took turns introducing themselves and welcoming Issi to the resistance. The small statured Cacique Enriquillo spoke last. What he lacked in physical stature, he certainly made up in wit, wisdom and warrior-spiritedness. When he spoke, he would nod as if trying to keep in step, in beat, with his own words. His eyes had a squinty quality to them, such that they seemed to barely open. As he sat cross-legged in the circle, he held his hands on his knees, arms supporting the weight of his torso. He leaned forward and spoke to each face, nodding, squinting, captivating.

"Welcome Issi!" begun Cacique Enriquillo.

"After the strange men landed on our shores, they killed my father and eighty other chiefs. The strange men

138

invited the chiefs to so-called peaceful talks but, in the end, they were burnt to death in a hut. All of them."

His squinty eyes closed even further, and his nodding stopped. He looked around the circle, not at anyone in particular. His face registered a muted pain. He took a deep breath as the sound of a wave dashed against the rocks outside.

He continued, in a laboured sigh, "And as if that was not enough, they killed most of the men, women and children who were at the meeting. I saw them cut our people open. I saw them cut off the fingers of our children. One by one. I saw them chop off heads of our people… and used the severed heads as weapons…. They beat old women with the heads of their sons and daughters."

Issi felt her baby move. It was not a kick, as she had grown accustomed to feeling, especially when she was in a happy mood. It just moved. It felt as though the baby was shivering. Ayanti felt it too, it seemed. She squeezed Issi's hand a little firmer.

"One of their priests raised me as his own child," continued Cacique Enriquillo.

"He felt that if I learned their language and about their god who died, I would be able to understand them and forgive and work with them to help our people to also forgive them."

The Cacique stood up. His face was no longer visible, and his words rolled out as echoes from somewhere beyond the darkness.

"Soon as I was old enough, I ran away with a few of my friends. We escaped to the mountains of Bahoruco."

Those were the mountains where Ayanti and the widow from our village had found refuge. Bahoruco represented the epicentre of the resistance. The fight against our oppression. When Ayanti arrived there, she struck up an immediate bond and friendship with Niti, the other woman in the cave.

"Niti reminded me of you Issi," Ayanti said.

"She tells me you are a warrior who knows no fear, dear Issi," whispered Niti, rubbing Issi's belly, looking dead and deeply into her eyes. There was an affection there that didn't yet have words. It was only, and could only be, felt.

In Bahoruco, Niti and Ayanti were in charge of growing the hot chillies that were dried and later weaponised into blinding powder missiles. The chili powder was used to fill clay balls which were hurled from slingshots into enemy territory. The powder would disperse in the wind or under the cover of darkness when the soldiers of the enemy were asleep, or too drunk to launch an effective defence or retaliate.

"I am from the island called Ay Ay, I am Kalinago," explained Niti.

"No, I am not an enemy," she responded, to the unspoken question written all over Issi's face.

"I was married to one of the chiefs who was burnt to death by them. His sister is married to my brother, still, I hope.... They are in Ay Ay."

Niti's marriage was one of those pacts between our peoples of the region, to make peace and share customs. Niti and her people were warriors. She was born to fight and knew the art of war.

The voice from beyond the darkness continued relating its painful tale: "One of them, raped my wife."

Cacique Enriquillo sat back down and re-joined the circle. He looked directly at Issi. He was not nodding. The waves paused their crashing and silence fell into the cave, like mute rays of sun.

"Issi, we have to kill them. All of them."

SAVAGE

***

I have experienced a few storms in my time. Not hurricanes or earthquakes though. That, however, was to change, on one of the strangest of days.

I had never seen anything like it before. There were scattered clouds in the sky. The sun ducked, almost playfully, in and out from behind them. Birds littered the sky, flying high in formation, in a hurry to get to destinations that existed only in my imagination. The horses neighed and stomped, and the noisy heavy-set cows mooed and sauntered restlessly across their corral. The evil dogs made sinister sounds, and no butterflies or small birds that used to raid the fruit trees, were anywhere in sight, that day.

The sea was calm until around the middle of the day when the wind picked up a few waves and flung them hard against the shore.

My mother told Paco that a hurricane was on its way, but he dismissed her, "then wave your bloody arms and stop it, since you know so much about the weather!"

Issi suggested that we make for the hills to sleep in a dry bat cave. My mother agreed but said only after things got worse, as they were sure to get. She told Padre Perez that a hurricane would hit, as the animals have issued a firm warning. He had no idea, nor did I, what a hurricane was, and what damage it could potentially wreak.

"My child do not be alarmed and do not alarm others with your musings," said Padre Perez, waving his amulet in the air.

By sunset, the sea was roaring mad and the animals that hadn't yet bolted, became noisier than ever. It started to rain, and as it poured down heavier and heavier it got darker and darker. The sky was securely blanketed behind giant black clouds, lit up now and again by huge streaks of lightning.

The sea rose higher and higher, the more the rain filled it up. Trees swayed until their tired roots gave way. Many huts did not last the night. Many of our people either escaped from the village in the raging storm, or simply died; either by drowning or hit by flying or falling debris. Some of Paco's men got carried away with the current as they futilely tried to secure their ships in the bay. No ships were left.

The wooden pillar, hoisted in the shape of a cross, was the only thing left standing as a reminder of the erstwhile existence of *la iglesia de san Francisco*.

Padre Perez found his last and ultimate refuge underneath the flooring of what he used to call, the altar. His swollen corpse was pulled out from under the rubble three full days after the hurricane had passed. Paco decided it was best to burn Padre Perez's body along with the remains of *la iglesia de san Francisco*. There was just not enough manpower to lift "that sack of sacred sludge," according to Paco, "so it's just as well we offer him up as a burnt sacrifice. Amen."

In many ways, I was relieved that the hurricane had come and solved some of our problems. Many of our people, for one, were liberated in one form or another. My mother was also relieved that her holy duties to Padre Perez were over. Issi was contemplative. And Paco was, expectedly, furious. He had lost most of his men. His ships were gone. He had no manpower and most of his documents and belongings were destroyed. He managed to salvage a couple barrels of wine and a large leather sack whose contents were unknown to me, at the time.

***

Don Andres Cervantes believed that a ship that was due to arrive from Castillia a few days before the hurricane struck, must have got caught in the storm and most likely been destroyed. Paco was in a state of agitated panic and as a result, moved swiftly through the wine he had salvaged during the hurricane. There were no servants to make anymore. And importantly, there were no crops, no maize, to make more wine.

"Don Paco, you have to calm down and keep your wits about you! There is no point losing it when we have lost everything already. It's time to gather ourselves and rebuild," counselled Don Cervantes.

"Don't tell me to calm down! Who do you think you are? The king, all of a sudden?!"

"No, Don Paco, all I am saying is that we have to keep a clear head..."

Paco interjected before Don Cervantes could finish. He drew his sword, gritted his teeth, and stuck the tip of the blade under Don Cervantes' nose, "One more word out of you Cervantes and I swear I will add you to the rubble of this stinking land!"

The land had indeed started to stink. The stench of death and decay was all around; inescapable. The odour settled and stayed like a stubborn horse, saddled but refusing to go anywhere. Corpses lodged in trees and vultures circled around them in enthusiastic anticipation.

Don Cervantes backed away from Paco and beckoned Issi to follow him.

Issi reluctantly dragged her heavy and hungry body up from the spot where she was sitting on a stump. Using her hand to support her back, she followed wearily behind Don Cervantes.

"Are we going somewhere?" asked Issi.

"I go where I want to go. You go where I want you to go. Just follow. Anything else?"

"Actually, yes. Just make sure this place you want to go is not too far, because I can't handle it…."

"You still got a mouth on you huh…never mind, I'll put it to better use."

Issi cast a sad, fatigued glance behind, gazing at me and my mother.

Moments after Don Cervantes and Issi left us, one loud shrill scream which ended in a deep hollow groan interrupted Paco's frantic monologue, which, up to that point, my mother and I had to quietly endure.

"Tinima and Lilia you have to pull more weight around here, so things can get back to normal as soon as possible! Someone has got to sort out the crops and someone has got to look for the animals that escaped. I mean both types, by the way! Those lazy bastards and the ones with hooves as well. I have to get word to Castillia and to get some ships back here. What's the use anyway? What use is a bloody ship when we have nothing to ship! We lost everything! I don't even know how or where to begin...Oh man! Can you smell that? Worse than a pauper's fart! Has it got hotter, you think? I'm melting here! So yeah, I expect you both to do more. A man's got to eat... Those damned fools...I don't know what they were even thinking, trying to save the damned ships. And this idiot Cervantes, can you believe the murderous, clepto of Cadiz! Blaming me! Bloody nerve! How the hell is it my fault? Bastard accused me! Me! Drunk! The nerve! I swear if...."

It was at that point that the shriek of a scream, abruptly punctuated Paco's tirade.

I made an instinctive dash towards the direction of the sound which spilled out from behind a pile of rocks and rubble situated not very far from where we were all gathered.

"Oh no! Oh no!" I screamed.

I ignored dirt, thorns and splinters, skidding on my knees to a sudden and bumpy stop, ramming into Issi's blood-soaked body, which had fallen at angle from atop the blood-drenched corpse of Don Cervantes.

Both bodies were joined together by the long, steely blade of Don Cervantes' sword. The handle was firmly clasped in Issi's grasp. Don Cervantes' was lying on his back, with his head tilted backwards, eyes wide open gazing skyward. Blood coursed slowly and deliberately out of the gap that caused his head to assume the angled position it rested in.

My mother threw her body onto Issi's bloody, lifeless form. She sobbed like day I was born.

Paco slowly loosened Issi's grip on the sword and tremblingly withdrew the sword, separating the two bodies. Issi body fell sideways hitting the ground with a thud.

There were two corpses, but three lives ended that day. Issi had made sure that the length of the blade not only severed her connection to this realm, but also ensured there was absolutely no chance that the child she carried would breathe a single breath.

Paco held me, and we wept together, shedding the tears his baby never would.

"I honestly don't think it's the best idea, Paco, but I'm sure you'll do what you will."

"Did I ask your opinion? And yeah, damn right I'll do what I want! Just get Lilia to set up my hammock. I am moving in with the two of you. It's better that way."

From the time Paco moved into our bohio, the constant battles between him and my mother raged furious and frequent.

"Can't you piss outdoors, or must you insist on living like an animal?!"

"I'll piss and shit and fart damn well where I please, thank you very much!"

"Okay, well that's it then! I'm done! Come Karaya, we're leaving! We will not live like this anymore…clear he's lost his mind and I've had enough! Enough! More than enough! Come!"

She marched towards door looking back to see me hesitating, "Child, come!"

I felt the bohio shake and the hairs on my arms woke up from their daydream. So did my feet as I hurried out behind her.

"Not so fast, bitch! Where the hell do you think you're going?" snarled Paco.

He raced towards the entrance and blocked it with outstretched arms and legs. A bogus grin was plastered over his face leaving me to wonder whether he had actually found the situation funny or whether he had in fact lost his mind. He rocked and swayed from side to side.

"Get out of my way Paco! Game over!" said my mother.

Paco leaned forward bending low enough to be face to face with my mother, rocking, swaying, grinning. His face was bright red. Dripping sweat.

"Enough, Paco! Enough!" said my mother.

I sensed a fury in her that was new to me. I did not recognise it. Paco broke out into an uncontrollable laugh, briefly losing his balance. He fell forward using his hands to break his fall. Dextrously, in a single motion, he scooped up two handfuls of dirt and swiftly released them into my mother's wide-open eyes.

Paco regained firm stance. Lifted his right foot and planted it square into my mother's belly. She balled up under the force of Paco's stomp. She rolled backwards till the thatched wall at the other end of the bohio stopped her.

"Don't you dare try it with me like that ever again, you hear me!"

My mother laid curled up on the floor. Paco advanced towards her. He towered over her and landed another kick to her abdomen. Then another. And another. Till I screamed for him to stop. Then he stopped.

He grabbed his large, brown, leather sack and shuffled through its contents emerging with a length of rope. He scooped my mother up like cargo and deposited her against the centre-pole of the bohio.

He tied her to the pole, spat at her and said, "Go ahead, try leaving now!"

Paco collapsed into the hammock and never moved for a whole day. My mother remained tied up and never moved for a period too long to even remember.

PHASE IV

THIS LAND

"We are all visitors to this time, this place. We are just passing through. Our purpose here is to observe, to learn, to grow, to love… and then we return home." – Australian Aboriginal saying

***

I must have collapsed from thirst and exhaustion from my nonstop sprint to escape the old village in search of Bahoruco and Cacique Enriquillo. The only things I remember carrying were the directions that Issi had planted in my head, plus Paco's heavy sword stuck to my hand by a crusty glue of dried up human blood.

My eyes opened to soft gleams of light, caressingly close to my face; like the morning sun summoning me to wake up. The warm glow of the two suns staring at me, got cut off by a sudden, involuntary blink. The loving gaze broke for a brief second. My own eyes widened in panic. But soon relaxed again, when a calm, soothing melody of a voice, accompanied by hands that cradled my face, wiping tears I only felt but never knew were there, whispered, "Welcome home my child. Welcome. I am Ayanti. I know your mother."

"Don't cry my dear, be happy. You're home!"

"Ayanti…?"

"Lift her up Mabo. See she's exhausted…"

It would seem I was not up to conversation, even though my spirit felt elated to have made the journey. I had no strength left. I barely stayed awake, till the sounds of drums woke me up.

Mabo had hoisted me onto his back and carried me into Bahoruco, Ayanti leading the way, singing. As she sung drums started to beat and dancers started to gather from out of nowhere. A large crowd gathered into what I could immediately identify from my mother's stories as the ceremonial square of her people, the batey.

I knew instantly what was happening. Young men ran into the middle of the square tossing and bouncing a ball around. Young girls with garlands of flowers danced and serenaded them…and me.

After a while I recognised the diminutive regal figure of Cacique Enriquillo entering the batey. He was carried by six muscular men atop his wooden four-legged duho which was masterfully carved in the shape of an iguana. The duho was stained black and adorned with bits of gold, around the eyes and along the back-rest.

Enriquillo wore an elaborate headdress of colourful feathers and two striking golden armbands which clung to his arms as though they were a natural part of the man himself.

He nodded at me as he was carried by. Ayanti lowered her gaze in respect and reverence. She stood next to me, holding my hand, "You are home my child."

After all the festivities, Ayanti and three other women, Niti was one of them, took me for a bath. They massaged my body with aromatic oils and scrubbed my skin with a mix of leaves and flowers. They gave me a warm brew to drink. This they said, would help me relax and restore my strength.

The whole session reminded me of the time my mother and Issi bathed me into womanhood. I cried and sobbed.

"My child, I'm not sure this bath will do you any good if you insist on moisturising with all that snot you're spewing out," said one of the women.

Ayanti rubbed my face and looked into my eyes. This made me uncomfortable and I knew she knew it too. She rubbed my belly with a handful of water.

"What did they do to you, my child, dear Karaya?"

It was one of those questions that did not require an answer. And one of those questions everyone knew signalled the start to a whole new private conversation. So, without a word, the other women respectfully granted Ayanti's wish for them to leave us two alone.

"How are Tinima and dear Issi, Karaya?"

The question was delivered by a pair of golden glares, that left me transparent. I knew, as did Ayanti, that I had nowhere to hide, nor could I hide anything, even if that was what I intended to do. Issi did tell me that Ayanti could not be deceived. That was my dilemma. How could I pull off the impossible?

I lied anyway.

"Issi is with the ancestors. And Paco killed my mother."

"Oh, I see," was her only remark. Her only comeback and invitation for me to carry on.

I told her how Issi and the child she was carrying met their end.

"Well done, Issi!" smiled Ayanti. Hardly the response I had anticipated.

What I did not tell her was the whole truth. The truth which had haunted me from the day I plotted it, to the very moment of recounting the horrid tale. I could not mention that I had warned Paco of the entire scheme that Issi and Ayanti and Enriquillo were putting together to take back the land. How could I?

***

"Is that true, Loca? Seriously? Or you're just trying to piss me off?!"

"Why would I make this up? Does it sound funny to you? Why would I want to upset you, when you already have enough in this place to keep you permanently pissed off?"

With that I pulled Paco's naked body closer to mine, sheltered from the sun under the guava shrubs that we had secretly formed into our own intimate haven, hidden and protected from it all.

"I don't want them to mess up our plan, Paquito!"

"Yeah, I get that, Loca. We will rule this land together…both of us. Together."

"I just don't know how I am going to tell Bibi about the baby. About us."

"No need to say anything. They'll see…and deal with it, or we'll deal with them. All of them, I don't care."

"Well sir, you'd better care...we talked about this."

"Indeed, we did..."

"The beatings I can understand and have even forgiven...but you have to keep your promise not to kill Bibi, ok?"

I remember him jumping to his feet to get dressed, pulling me up with him, into his arms.

"Soon, Loca. Soon," he said, rubbing my crumpled head of hair.

He got dressed and walked off, "Oh, Cervantes is going to take care of the Issi issue tomorrow."

If our plan were to ever succeed, we had to get rid of Issi. It was only necessary. Unfortunate but necessary. A necessary evil, Paco called it.

Of course I loved Issi! But I loved Paco more. He was more like me, and I was more like him.

"Look around Loca, your head doesn't have the fucked-up shape these idiots think is cute!"

And since no lady from Castillia was coming to be his bride, and we had this land, to ourselves, Paco said it was only right that we, both of us, *the de los Lobos*, stake our rightful claim.

We had to take out Issi. But that silly Cervantes forgot to save the child. Paco's child. That was the deal. Bloody fool, Cervantes.

***

Ayanti oiled my skin and brushed my hair. She gave me cotton loin cloths to wear. I thought of feigning grief and invoking tears, but I knew it was Ayanti, and none of that fooled her. I was also almost certain she knew the unspoken truth.

After I finished telling her about Issi's valiant departure, furnishing her deadpan remark, she prodded me on.

"And dearest Tinima…?"

This time I bawled and sobbed. The first time since I found my mother's stiffened body, tied to that pole in our last bohio. There was foam around her mouth and the sockets of her eyes were dark as night.

I of course did not mention this to Ayanti, because she would have known immediately that my mother had been poisoned. And she was.

Paco kept a jar of yuca poison in his leather sack. I had to guess that he used it on my mother, perhaps at a time when she might have asked for water to quench her thirst being tied to that pole in the baking bohio day after day.

The broken gourd I found next to the pole was evidence enough for me to see Paco's hand in my mother's death.

I single-handedly untied my mother's rigid corpse from the pole in the bohio and carried her over my shoulders to a patch beyond the new pineapple beds. I dug her grave, with my bare hands until they blistered and bled. I ignored the pain and did not shed a single tear. I cut off a lock of my mother's hair and braided it into mine before burying her in the shallow hole I managed to scratch out.

That night when Paco came to the bohio to sleep, in my hammock, next to me, he whispered, "Sorry Loca."

I did not utter a single word to him since he killed Bibi. I remember falling asleep while he tried, with kisses and cuddles to win some sort of forgiveness for breaking our pact.

"It was too much to handle, Lilia," Paco tried to explain at one point. "You know your mother can be a pain in the neck and I must admit that recently she really ramped it up a notch! You saw that, didn't you?"

I did understand. All too well. I knew my mother did not like Paco. Of course, she wasn't going to understand our love for each other. She wouldn't have understood that, given the way things had turned out, Paco and I had to be together. It was our destiny to rule this land. I knew she would have never agreed or understood. All the same, Paco had no right to kill her.

That was unforgiveable. That was just not part of the plan.

Besides, I had already sacrificed Issi, and Paco knew that as far as love goes, I loved Bibi the most.

"Yes, Paco! Of course, more than you! You're fine... but Bibi is Bibi. Kinda silly asking me to explain."

"Makes no sense, who would you replace me with then? Since Tinima is so irreplaceable...and I get that, she's your mother..."

"So, what's your stupid point? There are no other men in the land? Anywhere? Put it this way Paquito, let's not have to find out, ok!"

I wanted revenge, but I also wanted this land. I had to figure out a way how to get both.

One evening I made dinner, as usual, for Paco and the seven soldiers he had left. I added a deadly dose of Cohoba, the hallucinogen, to the seven soldiers' meals and put just enough into Paco's for him to be woozy but awake.

After the soldiers had fallen off one by one, I could see Paco trying to say something, or trying to summon his limbs to move, perhaps to grab me, to stop me, but he just laid there. A helpless spectator to all that was to happen next.

I called each soldier's name as I despatched them to wherever they went, after this life:

Jose Luis de Jesus

Pedro Guerrero Pacifico

Tomas Lorenzo Del Rio

Marco Morales De las Casas

Pablo Antonio Buendia

Santiago Salinas Trujillo

Salvador Santamaria

Each one entered his afterlife holding head in hand.

I could see sprinkles of pain covering Paco's face. It was somewhat amusing to see him like that. Paralysed. Not even his own words would obey him.

I stabbed the bloodstained sword in the ground next to Paco's cheek. Then I knelt beside him and curled up into a cuddle behind him.

I was tempted to say, "Don't worry, brother, husband, lover, father of my unborn child, I won't chop your pretty little head off. Your mother should at least be able to recognise you in the afterlife!"

But I didn't say a word. I just grinned and giggled and cuddled him. I loosened the lock of my mother's hair from my braids and slowly plaited the strands into a neat length of rope.

I thought, "Ok Paquito, I won't give you the pleasure of the memory of the sound of my voice, but I wish I could tell you that I hope you like the feeling of being tied...."

I rolled over and lapped my legs around Paco, sitting on his stomach. I wrapped the lock of my mother's hair turned rope around Paco's neck, and with the strength of the hands my mother did not possess, I sent Paco off to the land of his ancestors.

I remember thinking as his breathing slowed to a halt, "This land…is mine!"

***

"Tell me then Karaya, how are we going to deal with this?"

"With what?" I asked Ayanti, feigning ignorance, trying to ignore her eyes fixedly staring at my belly. She knew I was pregnant.

"Don't try to play games with me child!"

"I wasn't sure what you meant…"

"But now I am sure you are sure, sure?!"

I nodded in agreement.

If this witch can read minds, let her fucking read mine, I said to myself. If she thinks she's going to kill my child….

"What are you thinking Karaya? Or shall I call you Lilia? Eh? Which do you prefer?!"

"No, no, Karaya of course, that's the name my mother gave me, the name my people know me by."

"Your people? What people? And Lilia, isn't that a better name? More civilised, you said? Or what was it you said…?

"Said? Me? When?"

"Karaya, Lilia, whatever or whoever you are or want to be, I know who you are! You came here thinking you can trick these fools, these *salvajes,* as you called us, and take our land. Child, what have you done? What…who have you become? Who are you, really?"

The truth is I had no answers for her questions. Just rivers and oceans of tears of regret, sadness and loss.

That warm brew I was given during my bath with the women made me do much more than relax and rehydrate. The potion made everything so relaxed that the contents of my mind and my dreams poured out like water from a spring.

"We know you came here kill me, Karaya! What was it you said? You want to rip out my entrails and wear them as garlands, if I tried any funny business with you…!" She laughed so hard tilting her head back. Her hair flowed down her head in all directions.

"You are going to marry Enriquillo, huh? And rule the land, you said…." The laughter stopped and Ayanti's eyes glowed like burning coals.

"Listen to me child! This land will not be ruled. Not by you. Not by them. Not by anyone! Sure you…and the others who think they can, can try. But let me know when you succeed!"

It was night by the time Ayanti finished with me. I wanted to feel chided and ashamed. I also wanted to feel hopeful as I sat there resting in Ayanti's arms, her hands holding mine, both of us bathing in the blueish brightness of the light of the full moon.

*** The Beginning ***

Courtney J. Scott

GLOSSARY OF TAINO TERMS AND
HISTORICAL REFERENCES

Thanks

Thank you for reading and supporting my work.

Savage has been a journey worth taking and I am grateful to everyone who has encouraged and spurred me along. There were days when the savagery of writing, research, doubt, discouragement took their toll, but I stayed the course.

Thanks to Arleene and Kerri, the biggest cheerleaders of my writing. Thanks Chris for listening to my stories, when even I know, sometimes they make no sense. Thanks to Bettina, Jean-Paul, Fred and Nik for inspiration beyond words. Keion, Leith, Audrey, Cavell, Karen R-W, Eva, Yvonne, Dadland, Tanya, Logan, Leo, Gael, Hew, Toni, Russ, Dwight, Kori, Troy, Werner, Berneth, a massive thank you for your constant support!

To my students, who have become friends, who put up with my rambling and failed attempts at being funny, your constant check-ups on my progress, made me have to finish! Thank you!

Big thanks to my mother and my family, without whom the pages of my story would be blank.

About the Author

I am one big man, comprised of a million little bits, intent on fitting all the pieces together to complete this motley jigsaw of my life. Some ancestry DNA kit has confirmed that I am actually an assorted cocktail of all humanity. Really!

I write. Teach. Live.